JULIUS CAESAR

A BEGINNER'S GUIDE

JULIUS CAESAR

A BEGINNER'S GUIDE

ANTONY KAMM

Hodder & Stoughton

A MEMBER OF THE HODDER HEADLINE GROUP

Orders: please contact Bookpoint Ltd, 130 Milton Park, Abingdon, Oxon OX14 4SB. Telephone: (44) 01235 827720, Fax: (44) 01235 400454. Lines are open from 9.00–6.00, Monday to Saturday, with a 24-hour message answering service. Email address: orders@bookpoint.co.uk

British Library Cataloguing in Publication Data
A catalogue record for this title is available from The British Library

ISBN 0 340 84456 6

First published 2002
Impression number   10 9 8 7 6 5 4 3 2 1
Year 2007 2006 2005 2004 2003 2002

Cover photo by
Typeset by Transet Limited, Coventry, England.
Printed in Great Britain for Hodder & Stoughton Educational, a division of Hodder Headline Plc, 338 Euston Road, London NW1 3BH by Cox & Wyman, Reading, Berks.

CONTENTS

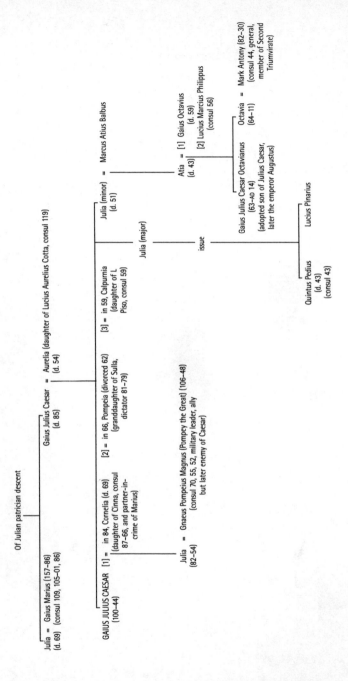

Genealogical chart of the family of Julius Caesar

Caesar – The Man in the Making 100–73 BC

He is said to have been tall, pale-complexioned, with a fine figure, rather full lips, and piercing black eyes. His health was good, though latterly he was liable suddenly to faint and also to have nightmares. Twice he had an epileptic fit during a military campaign. He was rather fastidious about his appearance. He had frequent shaves, and what hair there was on his head was regularly trimmed. It was rumoured that he had superfluous hair elsewhere on his body plucked out. He was acutely embarrassed by his baldness, which was a frequent subject of jokes on the part of his opponents. He took to combing his straggling locks forward from the back, and of all the honours heaped upon him by senate and people, the one he appreciated best and took advantage of most often was the privilege of wearing a laurel wreath at all times. He also dressed in a peculiar fashion. Instead of the short-sleeved, unbelted tunic which senators wore, his had long sleeves with a fringe at the wrists, with a belt loosely fastened round his waist.

Suetonius (AD 70–140), Roman historian, *Julius Caesar* 45

> *Perverted bedmates,*
> *   Caesar and Mamurra,*
> *Compete against each other*
> *   At serial adultery and*
> *Pulling teenage birds.*

Catullus (85–53 BC), Roman poet, LVII, 7–10

Most of the opposition forces who were captured alive, Caesar incorporated in his own legions. He granted amnesties to many of their leaders. Among them was [Marcus] Brutus, who later assassinated him.

Plutarch (AD 46–120), Greek historian, *Caesar* 46

The bald, bisexual dandy who is the subject of these contemporary or near-contemporary reports was born in the city of Rome on 12 July 100 BC or, according to some authorities, 102 BC. Julius Caesar came, on his father's side, from an upper-class family of illustrious origins but small material success – his father was a minor state official. The family belonged to the clan Julia, whose members claimed to be descended from Iulus, son of Aeneas, the mythical originator of the state of Rome. Aeneas was said to be the son of Anchises and of the goddess Venus.

> **KEY FACT**
>
> The original rulers of Rome were kings. Gradually the city became a state, whose top rulers were the two consuls. They were elected for one year only and had equal powers.

Caesar's mother's family, on the other hand, had come from small beginnings to hold positions of great power. Four of them, including Caesar's grandfather, had been consuls.

THE MARIUS CONNECTION

The marriage of Caesar's aunt Julia to Gaius Marius in 115 BC was to prove a mixed blessing. Marius (157–86 BC) was a soldier, who rose from obscurity to supreme power. He was originally elected consul in 108 BC, when he established Rome's first full-time professional army, paid out of the spoils of war, and introduced new army training methods. He managed to get himself elected consul five times, for the years 104–101 BC, but his ambition, the necessity to wage war in order to pay his army, and his lack of political understanding caused the government of Rome to be destabilized.

In 87 BC, having been forced to flee to Africa, Marius returned to Italy. With Cornelius Cinna (d. 84 BC), a former consul, he marched on Rome with an army which they collected on their way. There was a ghastly siege in which thousands died of plague. The city capitulated, its elders having extracted from Cinna a verbal undertaking that there would be no bloodshed. Marius, who took no active part in the negotiations, obviously felt that he was not bound by the promise. The killings went on for five days. Marius and Cinna now proposed themselves as consuls. No one dared oppose them. Marius died (it is said of drink), before he could take office. Cinna retained his consulship for the next three years until his death at the hands of his own troops.

Caesar would have been aged about 13 when his aunt's husband caused such slaughter in the city. When he was 15, and continuing his education, his father died. Shortly afterwards Caesar received an extraordinary double advancement in Roman society. He was already engaged to Cossutia, a young woman from a wealthy family, when Cinna proposed instead that Caesar should marry his daughter Cornelia. Caesar did not hesitate, and Cossutia was unceremoniously dumped. Cinna also appointed him priest of Jupiter, which was one of the three highest religious offices. That said, the post was hedged round with extraordinary taboos, as well as hazards. The priest of Jupiter was forbidden to ride a horse or see an army. He must not touch or even mention a nanny-goat, uncooked meat, ivy, or beans. He had to wear his pointy hat at all times, even indoors.

Meanwhile, Rome waited for the next political crisis. When it came, in 83 BC, Marius had unwittingly provided the means and the precedent.

KEY FACT

The Romans worshipped a multitude of gods, the chief of whom was Jupiter, who had a magnificent temple overlooking the heart of the city. He was regarded as the champion of the Roman people, to whom he was believed to bring success and wealth, as well as wisdom and health.

THE RULE OF SULLA

Cornelius Sulla (138–78 BC) had been elected consul for 88 BC, when he was also appointed to command the Roman forces against Mithridates, king of Pontus. Mithridates had invaded the Roman province of Asia and massacred 80,000 Roman and Italian citizens. After a successful campaign, Sulla returned to Italy in 83 BC. He had no official political position, but he commanded a trained army, and with this he threatened to take over the city of Rome itself. The consuls, one of whom was the 27-year-old Gaius Marius junior, adopted son of Caesar's aunt Julia and her husband, could raise only nominal resistance.

Sulla, effectively now in control of Rome and its empire in Italy and across the seas, had himself appointed not consul, but dictator, which gave him supreme power. His first act was to dispose of all political and personal opponents. He did this by using the novel method of proscription, the posting up in public of lists of his enemies. Anyone was now free to kill them, and would receive a reward for doing so. Over 1,600 prominent citizens were despatched in the first round of murders; more followed.

> Some of them, caught unawares, were killed where they were found, at home, in the street, or in the temple. Some were bodily heaved up from where they were and thrown at Sulla's feet. Some were dragged through the streets and kicked to death, the spectators being too frightened to utter a word of protest at the horrors they were witnessing. Others were expelled from Rome or had their property and belongings confiscated. Spies were everywhere, looking for those who had fled the city.
>
> Appian (second-century AD historian who wrote in Greek),
> *Civil Wars* I. 11

It was a bad time for Caesar, who was seen by Sulla as an enemy in that he was related by marriage to both Marius and Cinna. Sulla first tried to get Caesar to divorce his wife Cornelia, who had just given birth, or was about to give birth, to their daughter Julia. Caesar refused. Sulla responded by sacking him from his priesthood and confiscating his inheritance from his father and the money that Cornelia had brought him as a dowry when they married.

Caesar went into hiding from Sulla's secret agents. He changed his place of refuge almost every day, using the houses of friends where he could, or else bribing the householders. All this time he was suffering from what sounds to have been malaria.

Finally, a group of Caesar's relatives and supporters persuaded Sulla to grant him immunity from harassment. Sulla conceded grudgingly, with a remark that proved to be uncannily accurate: 'I give in! Have it your own way! But remember that the man you are so keen to save will one day destroy the cause of the ruling party which you and I are trying to uphold. There are many signs of Marius in Caesar.'

Caesar took the opportunity to remove himself offered by a military appointment abroad, as aide to Marcus Thermus, governor of the Roman province of Asia Minor. As one of his assignments he was sent to the neighbouring Black Sea coastal kingdom of Bithynia to pick up a fleet of ships which was anchored there. While Caesar was enjoying the hospitality of Nicomedes III, king of Bithynia, Nicomedes enjoyed Caesar's homosexual favours. The affair returned to haunt Caesar in later years, when his soldiers sang bawdy songs about it.

Caesar redeemed himself and his reputation, however, in his first action, at the storming of the coastal town of Mytilene on the island of Lesbos. For saving the life of a comrade, Thermus awarded him the citizen's crown, the highest award for bravery. The crown itself, a wreath of oak leaves, was worn on civic occasions, notably at public shows and the games. When anyone wearing it put in an appearance, the whole audience rose to their feet.

KEY FACTS

Malaria is caused by mosquitoes, for which there was plenty of scope in ancient Rome. The original settlement was built on the top of the Palatine Hill, conveniently situated by the River Tiber. The surrounding land, however, on which the rest of the city was constructed, was swampy and liable to flooding. The network of sewers which took the waste away from the communal loos and the ground floors of apartment blocks, provided further health hazards. So did the streets themselves, with their dungheaps and open drains, into which people poured the contents of their chamber-pots.

Back in Rome, Sulla, after completing the purge of his political opponents, reorganized the constitution to return the power if not actually to the people, at least to the upper classes of the people. He also reformed the legal system. This done, he gave up office and retired to his country estate in Campania to write his memoirs. In 79 BC, two days after he had finished his book, he died of an infestation of lice.

THE RISE OF JULIUS CAESAR

Caesar now returned to Rome. He had recently turned 21, and was already looking to make a name for himself. The stage was set for a further revolution against Sulla's reforms, but Caesar decided not to throw in his lot with Marcus Lepidus, one of the consuls for 78 BC, who instigated the opposition. Lepidus and his now irregular army were defeated twice in 77 BC. Lepidus was outlawed and fled to Sardinia, where he sickened and died, not, it is said, because of his public failure, but of a broken heart: he had discovered a letter to his wife written by her lover.

Caesar was biding his time, while polishing his forensic skills. (There is nothing new in those who seek positions of political influence starting their careers in the law courts.) He decided that it would be good for his image to instigate and conduct the prosecution of Gnaius Cornelius Dolabella, a former consul, for extortion while governor of the province of Macedonia. The case failed, but Caesar did himself no harm, because he was now asked to take on the prosecution of Gaius Antonius, an officer who, it was alleged, had enriched himself unlawfully at the expense of cities in Greece during the war against Mithridates. He won the case in court, but lost it on appeal. Possibly because both Dolabella and Antonius had been prominent supporters of Sulla, Caesar now thought it wise to go abroad, ostensibly to study the art of public speaking on the island of Rhodes under the eminent Apollonius Molon.

On the way to Rhodes, following the coast of Asia Minor, his ship was captured by pirates off the island of Pharmacusa. They demanded a ransom of 20 talents of silver for his release – a Greek talent weighed 26.24 kilos. Caesar said he was worth far more than that, and instructed his crew to go around the neighbouring towns and raise 50 talents, while he remained prisoner, attended by his doctor and two valets. The pirates, from Cilicia, were a bloodthirsty lot, but this did not worry Caesar. He joined in their sports and practised his public speaking on them. Any hecklers he promised to hang in due course. The pirates took this as a great joke.

When, after a month, the ransom money arrived, Caesar paid it over, obtained his freedom, and sailed for the nearby port of Miletus. There he hired a squadron of light ships, and returned to Pharmacusa, where he found the pirate fleet still at anchor. He took the pirates prisoner, captured several of their ships, and relieved them of their money and booty. He then secured the men in prison in Pergamum, the capital of the province, and asked Junius, Thermus's successor as governor, what should be done with them. When Junius dithered, thinking he might make some money by ransoming the prisoners to their families or associates, Caesar took it upon himself to have them crucified, as he had threatened he would. Being of a merciful disposition, he first had their throats cut.

He was in Rhodes in 74 BC when Mithridates once more set his armies against the Roman people in Asia. Nicomedes had just died, without an heir, bequeathing his kingdom to Rome. Mithridates sent a small force into Bithynia, thinking it would be easy to wrest the territory from its new owners. When Caesar heard about this, he crossed over to the mainland, raised a body of troops locally, and drove Mithridates's force back into its own territory. Then he resumed his studies in Rhodes.

Caesar sailed for Rome again in 73 BC, having learned that he had been appointed a priest of the pontifical college. These priests, 15 in number, were the administrators and organizers of religious affairs, and the authorities on the calendar and festivals. It was a political office in that all matters relating to religion were also matters of state. To a young man of Caesar's social class, the only careers open to him were the army, the law, and politics. He had seen action both on the battlefield and in the courts. Now he set his sights on a political future – but he would achieve it in his own way and on his own terms.

Caesar's World 2

The man who appears to me to be properly alive, and to enjoy life, is engaged in something constructive, and seeks recognition by some famous deed or the exercise of a useful art. It is a glorious thing to be of service to the state, nor is eloquence to be despised. A man may achieve fame in peacetime or in war.

Sallust (86–35 BC), Roman historian, *Catiline* II–III

Traditionally, Rome is said to have been founded on 21 April 753 BC, and would thus have been about 650 years old when Caesar was born. The glittering civilization of Greece went back even further, but Greece had been conquered and became a Roman province in 146 BC, though the influence of its culture pervaded Roman life. As the Roman poet Horace (65–8 BC) put it rather disrespectfully: 'Greece may have lost the war, but she took her uncouth conquerors in hand, and introduced her ancient culture to the bumpkins of Rome' (*Epistles* II 1, 156–7).

THE ROMAN CONSTITUTION

Unlike the Greek model, republican Rome was never a proper democracy, nor was it a classless society. The state was dominated by the two upper classes: the senators, who qualified by birth, wealth, or position, and the equestrians or knights, whose wealth had to be above a certain level. There was a further divide between the patricians, members of the ancient aristocratic families (such as was Caesar's) who had dominated Roman politics since the inception of the republic, and the *plebs*, the common people. The *plebs* were subdivided according to whether they were freeborn or former slaves, citizens of Rome or from the surrounding parts. During the time of Caesar, it is probable that one in three of the congested population of the city of Rome was a slave.

So far from being a democracy, the constitution had evolved to the extent that it was very difficult for anything constructive to be done at all. The functions of the two consuls (one of whom was normally a plebeian) were largely formal. Sulla doubled the numbers in the senate to 600 by introducing into its membership equestrians, men from outside Rome, and former state officials. The senate was, however, principally an advisory body, but had nominal control over finance, administration of the state and empire, and foreign relations. Individuals who carved out for themselves positions of real power, and had enough wealth, simply ignored the senate, as Marius and Sulla had done, and Caesar would do.

Responsibility devolved on four assemblies. Voting was by group or category; the majority decision within a group represented one vote. The *comitia curiata* (assembly of wards or courts) was drawn from the three original tribes of the city. The *comitia centuriata* (assembly of centuries), consisted of 193 groups of citizens of Rome, allocated according to their means. Each century could contain any number of members, but 98 of the votes (a majority) were vested in the 18 centuries of equestrians plus the 80 comprising the top five property bands. The *comitia centuriata* could declare war. It also elected senior government officials. The *comitia tributa* (assembly of tribes) elected lesser officials. Any citizen was entitled to attend meetings of the *comitia centuriata* and *comitia tributa* and to cast his vote in the group to which he belonged. The *concilium plebis* (popular assembly) also voted by tribes, but patricians were excluded from membership. The powers which over the years the *concilium plebis* arrogated to itself, by collective bargaining or strike action, were considerable. Decrees were binding on the whole community, and its elected officers, the tribunes of the people, were empowered to hold up any business of state by invoking a power of veto.

Those who aspired to legitimate power ran for a series of public offices: quaestor, aedile, praetor, censor, and the ultimate goal, consul. This sequence was known as the *cursus honorum*, the race (or course) of honours. Sulla re-applied the regulation that there should be a ten-year gap between holding the same office twice, and established the rule that there should be two years between holding an office and being elected to the next higher one up the ladder.

Elections to the office of censor, reserved for men of very high rank in the senate, were held every five years. Other officials served for a year. Consuls had normally served previously as praetors.

RELIGIOUS PRACTICES

To the Romans, religion was a contractual relationship between humans and the spiritual forces which governed their existence and well-being. This operated on two levels – domestic and official. In the home, the head of the family supervised the rituals. The senate acted as the state's intermediary between the population and the gods. The post of *pontifex maximus*, the head priest of the religion of the state, was an elected office, held for life. His principal political function was to decide which days in the year were favourable or unfavourable for conducting public business.

> **KEY FACTS**
> **Cursus honorum**
> CENSOR (2): chief registrar, finance and tax officer, inspector of public works, governor of public morality
> PRAETOR (6): chief law officer and judge, deputy to consul. Provincial governors were normally ex-consuls or former or serving praetors.
> AEDILE (4): supervisor of public works, also games.
> QUAESTOR (20, minimum age 25): assistant to consuls, controller of finances, keeper of records.

The Romans collected their deities, rituals, traditions, and superstitions from a variety of sources. Many of their gods and goddesses had their equivalents in Greek religion or mythology. The Roman absorption with taking omens, by examining the entrails of sacrificed animals, or by observing natural or unusual phenomena, was derived from the Etruscans, who, with the Latins, occupied the region before the foundation of the city of Rome. Omens were sought, and appropriate action taken, before a decision was made on almost any matter of state or in the home. The Romans also practised animism, imbuing natural phenomena, trees, water, caves, animals, and even articles of furniture, with spiritual powers.

Prayer was fundamental to belief, and was often accompanied by some form of sacrifice or offering. This made much sense to the Romans, for the object of their prayers was to obtain material advantages. The more expensive and elaborate the sacrifice, the greater would be the benefits.

Julius Caesar, as befits a realist in war and an opportunist in politics, was not averse to enjoying the material proceeds of religious office, while in practice taking little notice of the implications of the rituals. He went into battle whether or not the sacred chickens had eaten their grain, or whatever colours the calves' livers were. On one occasion, when a priest reported that the sacrificial beast was missing a heart, he observed: 'The omens will be more favourable when I wish them to be.' Famously, though, he ignored to his cost the numerous phenomena which it is said forecast his death.

THE ROMAN ARMY

Marius was primarily responsible for turning the citizen army of Rome into the professional fighting force that his nephew Caesar was to exploit so effectively. The Romans could be utterly ruthless and bloodthirsty in the interests of organization, and when it came to imposing their own brand of civilization, which they saw as beneficial, on conquered peoples. It was a vicious circle! The Romans needed armed forces to protect them from incursions by peoples outside the boundaries of Roman influence. Armed forces had to be paid. In the ancient world, a soldier's rewards were the spoils and loot of a conquering army. The acquisition of provinces turned Rome from a city-state into an empire, which in republican times expanded according to circumstances or as the senate decreed. Outside the widening boundaries of her territories were more hostile peoples, sometimes several of them threatening the peace in different parts of the Roman world at the same time. The Roman economy depended on slavery. Conquered peoples ensured a ready supply of slaves, at a time

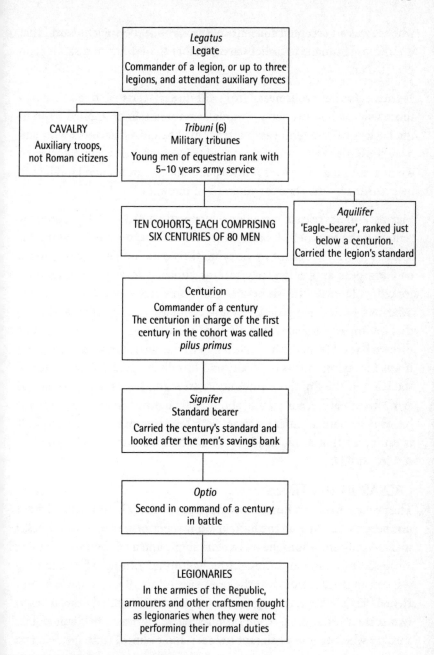

The Roman Legion in late republican times

when it was an accepted convention throughout the ancient world that it was more humane to inflict slavery, rather than death or disabling, on defeated enemies.

Marius recruited volunteers from the lowest class of free citizens – those who had no property – though in doing this he applied a rod to the backs of those who came after him. The citizen-farmers who had been the basis of previous armies had their own land to which to return when a campaign was over. The urban poor had none, and land had to be provided by the state for veterans of the wars.

Marius also increased his army's manoeuvrability on the march by reducing the number of camp followers and wagons, and making his soldiers more self-reliant by carrying their own kit, entrenching tools, cooking pots and emergency rations attached to their persons on a forked pole over the shoulder. From this, they got the nickname 'Marius's Mules'. He redesigned the standard weapon, the javelin, so that on impact its shaft came off, thus preventing it being dislodged or thrown back. He made the eagle emblem the chief standard of a legion; it was the legion's focus of loyalty and its rallying point. The legion was the basis of the Roman army, and its strength. It was a self-contained army in miniature, containing about 5,000 fighting men. Caesar fought his wars in Gaul at different times with between four and 12 legions. It is estimated that at his death in 44 BC the total number of legions in service was 37.

CAESAR IN HIS TIMES

The average freeborn Roman was not a particularly hard worker; he did not need to be, since all the hard grind was performed by slaves. Caesar was not only ambitious, he was a workaholic and a perfectionist: he was 'obsessed by action and thought he had done nothing while anything was left to do', according to the poet Lucan (AD 39–65: *The Civil War*, II, 656–657). When campaigning in Gaul, Caesar dictated despatches to two secretaries at once while on horseback. He was a brilliant public speaker who became a brilliant military and political strategist. He was a gambler, who would spend money he did not have to achieve his ends. He was also a prolific writer with a distinctive literary style.

Caesar's all-round abilities surprised his opponents, as sometimes they may have surprised even himself. One of his party tricks was to guess the value of a pearl by weighing it in the palm of his hand. He was an avid collector of *objets d'art* and also of slaves, particularly those of handsome appearance and more-than-average attainments. He was also an avid womanizer, whose mistresses, it was said, included several queens. Yet he was, on the whole, fair to his own womenfolk at a time when women were generally subject to male authority of one kind or another for the whole of their lives. He refused to divorce his first wife at Sulla's command. When his aunt, the widow of public enemy Marius, died, he had images of her husband carried in the funeral procession, and delivered a moving speech over her body. It was usual for there to be funeral orations for elderly women. When, in the same year, his young wife Cornelia died, Caesar created a precedent by giving her an oration too. He was loyal to his mother, a Roman matron of the old, severe, school, and had her to live with him from the time he had a home of his own until her death. He ate frugally when on campaign, but indulged himself on other occasions. One of his hosts wrote that, having bathed and been anointed with oil, Caesar was able, by taking emetics, to 'eat and drink to excess, and with obvious enjoyment' (Cicero to Atticus, 19 December 45 BC).

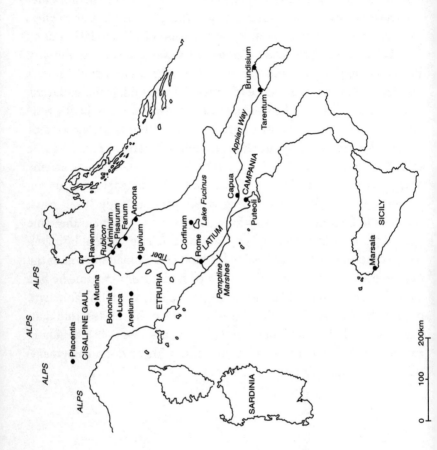

Map 1 Italy

Caesar – The Politician 72–59 BC

As Caesar was crossing the Alps [to take up his appointment in Spain], it is said that he passed a wretched village, occupied by a few barbarians. His companions made a joke of it: 'Could it be that here too there is rivalry for office, enmity over who should take precedence, and jealousy against each other among men of power?' To which Caesar answered, quite seriously, 'I would rather be first among these people than second in Rome.'

Plutarch, *Caesar* 11

Caesar began his political career as a military tribune. Since his year of duty coincided with the slave revolt of Spartacus in 72 BC, it is likely that he took part in that campaign and served under the man appointed to lead it, the enormously rich Crassus. Six thousand slaves survived the final battle. Crassus crucified them all the way along the road from Rome to Capua, where the revolt had started. He also, in the course of the campaign, revived the ancient punishment of decimation for the 500 of his own men who had disobeyed his orders, singling out one in every ten for public execution before the whole army.

KEY FACT

Marcus Licinius Crassus (d. 53 BC) bought up cheap, from the state, the estates of those who had been proscribed by Sulla. He also, at the first sign of a fire in the city, used to make a nominal offer not only for the burning house, but for all those in the vicinity. He then had them refurbished by his team of 500 craftsmen slaves, and sold them at a profit or let them at exorbitant rents.

Crassus was elected consul for 70 BC, with 'Pompey the Great', a born military leader, who was under the statutory age for the post and had never held any official position in the state.

Caesar, too, was now campaigning for public office, and was elected quaestor for 68 BC, which also gave him a seat in the senate. He served his quaestorship in Spain, but demanded to be recalled after sensing his destiny during a visit to Cadiz, where he came across a statue of Alexander the Great. 'He gave a hearty sigh, as if disgusted with his own lack of direction in having done nothing at an age at which Alexander had already conquered the world' (Suetonius, *Julius Caesar* 7).

Three years after the death of Cornelia, Caesar married Pompeia, a granddaughter of Sulla. She was well connected and she was rich, two qualities to appeal to an ambitious man who was already heavily in debt. The best way to catch the eye of the electorate was to spend money on public works and entertainment, and Caesar's financial position worsened during a stint as curator of the Appian Way, which linked Rome to the south. Any improvements to the facilities which were not covered by the state's allocation of funds, came out of the curator's own pocket. The next official step up the political ladder was the post of curule aedile, which he achieved in 65. The two curule aediles were not only responsible for orderly behaviour in the streets and markets of the city, and for the maintainance of temples and other public buildings, but were obliged personally to finance the games and other shows which the public expected. Caesar's provision of games, theatrical performances, processions, and public

banquets was both lavish and liberal. Somewhat belatedly, he mounted a games in honour of his father, who had died 20 years earlier. An unprecedented number of pairs of gladiators (some say 320) fought each other to the death, all wearing silver armour.

KEY FACTS

Gnaeus Pompeius Magnus (106–48 BC) raised his own army in support of Sulla, and defeated Marius in Africa. In 67 BC he rid the Mediterranean of pirates in just three months, taking 20,000 prisoners, most of whom he converted to agricultural pursuits. In 66 he defeated Mithridates and annexed Asia Minor. He conquered Syria in 63 and, having entered Jerusalem, made Judaea subservient to Syria's Roman governor.

Alexander (356–323 BC), king of Macedonia, succeeded his father in 338 BC as commander of the forces of Greece against Persia, whose king he defeated in 333 and 331. Having overrun the Persian empire, he continued east into India. He was taken ill and died on the return journey, having spread the Greek language and culture through the eastern world.

Since he had spent all his wife's money, as well as his own, it is probable that Caesar was now heavily involved with Crassus, whose avariciousness extended to money lending on a vast scale. Crassus was quite capable of buying in some of his client's debts, and holding them against the time when Caesar could repay him from the profits he would eventually make as a provincial governor. Caesar was now 35. He was ambitious for political advancement; it had also become an economic necessity.

ELECTIONS, CONSPIRACY, AND SCANDAL

The consuls in 63 were Cicero and Caesar's former adversary, Gaius Antonius. The campaign the previous July had been hard and vicious. Cicero had no money with which to bribe the electorate, so he relied on his forensic skills to blacken his opponents. In the case of Lucius Sergius Catilina (Catiline), who had stood before and failed to be elected, this was not difficult. Catiline had been served with notice of trial for extortion when he was governor of Africa in 67. He was also under suspicion for several murders, including that of his own son, conspiring against the state, and having sex with a vestal virgin. Cicero was elected by an overwhelming majority, to serve with Gaius Antonius as the other consul. Cicero made a deal with Antonius. In return for being allowed to exercise sole power, he made over to him the rich province of Macedonia which was Cicero's post-consular privilege.

> **KEY FACT**
>
> Marcus Tullius Cicero (106–43 BC) was *novus homo*, the first of his family to achieve public office, and thus regarded as an upstart. He had built up a formidable reputation in the courts of law as a defending and prosecuting advocate. He served as quaestor in Sicily in 75 and praetor in 66.

There were further significant elections in 63 BC. On the death of the incumbent *pontifex maximus*, Caesar offered himself for election as his successor and, against all the odds, succeeded, mainly by extensive bribery of the electorate. He saw the post and its perks, which included an extensive house in the Via Sacra, as a further opportunity to exert political influence, and he gambled everything on it. As he left his home in Subura, an unprepossessing district of the city where provisions were sold and prostitutes plied their trade, his mother, in tears, went with him to the door. He kissed her goodbye and said, 'Today I shall be *pontifex maximus* or an exile for ever.'

Later in the year, in October, Catiline stood again as a candidate for the consulship and, once again, failed to be elected.

Caesar further consolidated his position on the political ladder by being elected praetor for 62. Catiline, on the other hand, baulked for the third time of his goal, mounted a coup to overthrow the state. It was said that he bound his fellow conspirators into the plot by killing a boy and pronouncing an oath over the entrails, which they all then ate. The basic plan had been laid down some time earlier for just such an eventuality. Gaius Manlius, who had been a centurion in Sulla's army, would raise a military force in Etruria, to the north of the city, ready to march on Rome. Publius Cornelius Lentulus Sura, a former consul who had subsequently been expelled from the senate, but was now back in office as praetor, would instigate a riot in the city and organize the assassination of Cicero and other leading members of the establishment. Catiline would appear as if in response to the needs of both his supporters and his opponents, and be appointed dictator.

The plot failed because one of the leading conspirators, Quintus Curius, blabbed to his high-born mistress Fulvia, that he would shortly be in the money, thus hoping to retain her affections at a time when her interest in him was on the wane. She extracted some information from him and leaked it to members of the senate. Crassus went straight to Cicero with the evidence, and Cicero acted.

He called a meeting of the senate, and obtained the necessary powers to proceed against the conspirators once sufficient evidence had been gathered. Catiline was allowed to join his army in Etruria. Lentulus and four others were arrested. Cicero convened the senate to discuss what should be done with them. In his opening speech he indicated that he favoured the death penalty. The consuls elect and ex-consuls agreed with him. Caesar was then called upon to speak. At the close of a long, carefully argued address, he proposed instead that the estates of the accused should be confiscated, and that they should be imprisoned for life in various of the bigger towns in Italy.

When it seemed that Caesar's oratory had swung the vote, Cato, tribune of the *plebs*, stood up. Cicero had taken the precaution of discreetly disposing around the senate-house a number of his slaves who were skilled shorthand writers, so that he had a written record of the speech. Predictably, Cato advocated death for the conspirators, while attacking Caesar for offering leniency to those who aimed to subvert the state by terrorism. Cato halted in his harangue when he saw a folded note being brought in and handed to Caesar. He demanded that Caesar read it out. Instead, Caesar passed it to him. It was a letter of encouragement to Caesar from his current, and for some time favourite, mistress, Servilia, who was Cato's half-sister. Cato flung it back at him and resumed speaking.

KEY FACT

Marcus Porcius Cato (95–46 BC), 'Cato the Younger', was born in Utica. A stern moralist, and zealous orator, he was staunchly opposed to Caesar.

The sentence was confirmed as death. The accused were collected from the praetors' homes where they had been kept under house arrest. Cicero himself accompanied Lentulus to the state prison, where Lentulus was let down into a small, stinking dungeon, and strangled. Then the other four were executed, one by one, in the same manner. It was Cicero's finest hour.

When the news reached Etruria, many of Catiline's soldiers melted away. The rest were finally hunted down, and slaughtered, Catiline with them.

Caesar's spell of office as praetor in 62 was eventful. While Catiline was still at large, Caesar was suspended from his duties by the senate for supporting a motion that Pompey should be recalled from the east with his army to restore order. He took off his praetorian robe, dismissed his lictors, the guards who walked in front of officials of state carrying the symbols of power, and went home. A noisy crowd demonstrated, probably not spontaneously, in favour of his reinstatement. Caesar went out and begged them to desist. The senate, won over by his dignified behaviour, asked him to resume his office.

The festival of Bona Dea, the 'good goddess', was celebrated in the first week of December each year at the house of a senior officer of the state. It was a mystical ceremony, involving secret rites, and strictly for women only. In 62, the venue was the official residence of Caesar, in his capacity of *pontifex maximus*. Publius Clodius, a notorious upper-class lout, decided to infiltrate the ceremony in drag. Some said it was because he fancied Caesar's wife Pompeia, who was in charge of the proceedings, but it was equally likely to have been done as a prank. He was discovered, recognized, and thrown out of the house. There was a fine rumpus! Caesar promptly divorced Pompeia. Clodius was haled into court on a charge of sacrilege. Caesar refused to testify against him. When asked by the prosecutor why, then, he had divorced Pompeia, he replied enigmatically: 'My wife must not even be thought to be under suspicion.' Cicero, called to the witness stand, demolished Clodius's alibi, for which Clodius never forgave him. Crassus bribed the jury, and Clodius was acquitted.

THE REIGN IN SPAIN

Caesar's next post was that of governor of Further Spain, for which he would have departed much sooner had his creditors not impounded his carriage and wagon train. He was saved from embarrassment by Crassus, who paid the necessary bills. Once in Spain, Caesar gave less thought to public business or the administration of justice, than to the acquisition of money to pay off Crassus and settle other debts, and military glory to support his claim to the consulship for 59. He was successful on both counts. Indeed, he made so much money from booty, tribute, and by other means that he sent some back to the public treasury in Rome, and bolstered the pay packets of his legionaries and the auxiliary soldiers whom he enlisted locally.

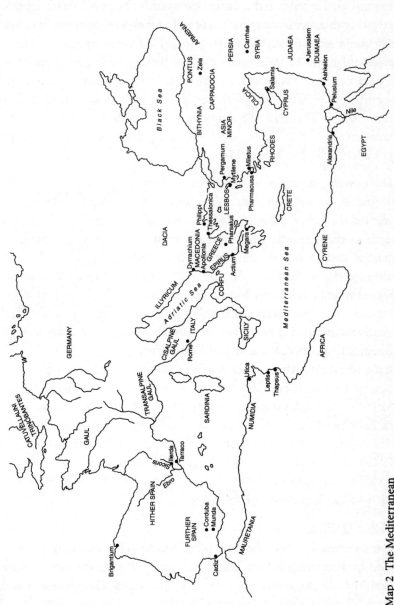

Map 2 The Mediterranean

On the military front he discovered his talent for large-scale operations. He mounted a campaign against the province's brigands, defeating them by a combination of military and naval operations, and relieving them of their booty. He showed off the strength of Rome in places inhabited by independent local tribes, including Brigantium on the north coast. There was no military glory to be got from peaceful submission, so wherever there was the slightest excuse, he destroyed their towns. Then, in the summer of 60, without waiting for his successor to arrive, he set off back home, bent on announcing his candidature for the consulship.

There were, however, one or two technical problems to be overcome. The senate had granted Caesar a triumph for his campaign against the Spanish brigands. A victorious general had to remain outside the city limits until the day of his triumph if he was to retain his command. To qualify for election he had to register his candidature personally in Rome. Since Pompey had already tried to stand for the consulship *in absentia*, and had been refused,

> **KEY FACT**
>
> The term candidate comes from the Latin *candidatus*, 'clothed in glittering white'. Romans offering themselves for election to public office made their togas extra white with chalk.

there was no way that Caesar would be allowed to register by proxy. He bowed to the inevitable, and presented himself in person, thus forfeiting his command and his triumph. The senate retaliated in a rather childish manner. As consular colleague, Caesar was lumbered with Marcus Calpurnius Bibulus, whom he hated – Bibulus was also Cato's son-in-law. Then the senate blocked Caesar's way to rich pickings after his consulship by assigning him, as his province, the care of 'woodlands and mountain pastures'.

THE CONSUL

Caesar's first act when he took office was to get Pompey fully behind him by proposing a land bill which would enable the settlement of Pompey's veterans from his eastern campaigns. His second was to establish an understanding with Pompey and Crassus, that none of them would take any political action of which either of the others disapproved. This informal alliance is known as the First Triumvirate, literally, 'rule (or board) of three men'. Caesar had the charisma and popular appeal, Crassus the money, and Pompey his troops. Cicero was invited to join them, but refused, thus putting himself in the wrong with all three.

Caesar further bound Pompey to him by giving him his daughter Julia in marriage, though she was already engaged to someone else. Julia was Pompey's fourth wife and, though she was over 20 years younger than him, it was a happy marriage, prematurely ended by her death five years later.

Business in the senate became farcical. Instead of following the rules of precedence, Caesar would call on either Crassus or Pompey to open the proceedings. Determined to push through his land bill, he had Cato arrested for attempting to talk it out by filibustering. Cato was released only because so many members of the senate chose to accompany him to jail. Caesar now took the bill to the popular assembly, of which his crony, Publius Vatinius, was tribune. An attempt by Bibulus to intervene while Caesar was speaking was met by armed force. He was physically abused and had a basketful of dung tipped over him.

The next day Bibulus called a meeting of the senate to get a state of emergency declared. When he failed in this, he resorted to the ingenious tactic of announcing that the omens were unfavourable, thus ensuring that business was suspended. Caesar ignored the interruption. Bibulus retired to his house for the remainder of the session, ostensibly to watch the sky for further phenomena. This left Caesar free to act on his own for the rest of the year. Various jokes circulated, such as signing off spoof documents with the phrase, 'Executed in the consulship of Julius and Caesar'.

Not that all Caesar's legislation was self-seeking. In particular he promoted a law ensuring that provincial citizens could initiate prosecutions where they felt that they had been subjected to extortion;

it remained in force for several hundred years. But when all is said and done, his principal objectives were to secure his future as potential leader of the state, and to ensure that he could not be prosecuted for any malpractice during his year of office. He and Pompey decided that the consuls for the next year would be Aulus Gabinius and Lucius Calpurnius Piso, who were duly elected. Gabinius, as tribune of the people in 66, had presented the law conferring on Pompey the command of the campaign against the pirates. Piso, according to contemporary accounts, was an unprincipled debauchee who, during his post-consular office as governor of Macedonia, shamelessly exploited his post. He was also Caesar's father-in-law, for in 59 the consul had married Piso's daughter, Calpurnia.

It was Vatinius, in the popular assembly, who fixed Caesar's chosen command, governor of Cisalpine Gaul (that is, Gaul 'this side of the Alps') and Illyricum for a period of five years. Since there could be no Roman troops in Italy south of the river Rubicon, which marked the border with Cisalpine Gaul, whoever governed the province effectively commanded the rest of Italy too. If Caesar wanted military prestige, Illyricum offered a take-off point for attacking the troublesome Dacians. Then there came a stroke of luck for Caesar, such as happens to great men. The tribes beyond the province of Transalpine Gaul (roughly corresponding to Provence and Languedoc), began massing for trouble, among themselves and with Rome. Metellus Celer had been appointed governor of Transalpine Gaul, with a brief to prosecute the war against the tribes if necessary. He died on his way to take up his post. Pompey successfully argued in the senate that Caesar should take on Metellus's command as an additional responsibility.

Caesar had one more piece of business to conduct before marching off to glory. He

KEY FACT

Quintus Caecilius Metellus Celer came from a distinguished plebeian family. He had been praetor in 61, and an unforgiving consul in 60, when he distin-guished himself in the field by cutting off Catiline's escape route. He was married to the profligate Clodia, sister of Clodius and mistress of Catullus, who calls her Lesbia in his verse.

needed someone in the popular assembly to replace Vatinius, whose term of office as tribune ended in 59: preferably someone as ruthless and audacious as Caesar was himself. His choice fell on the odious Publius Clodius. The fact that Clodius was a patrician, and therefore ineligible, was no problem. Caesar, as consul and *pontifex maximus*, had Clodius formally adopted by a plebeian, Publius Fonteius, who was younger than his adoptive son.

Clodius performed his duties to perfection. He introduced a law by which anyone who had executed a Roman citizen without trial should be outlawed. That took care of Cicero, who went into voluntary exile in Thessalonica. Clodius then ordered the annexation of Cyprus, and had Cato posted there as governor. With his two most eloquent and able adversaries out of the way, Caesar was able with greater peace of mind to pursue his elaborate vision of himself at the centre of the known world.

4 Caesar – The General 58–49 BC

In less than ten years in Gaul, Caesar successfully stormed over eight hundred cities, subdued three hundred tribes, and fought hand-to-hand battles against a total of three million warriors, of whom he killed a million, and took as many more prisoner.

Plutarch, *Caesar* 15

The predominately Celtic tribes of Gaul maintained a loose, sometimes adversarial, relationship with each other. Though they had not developed the art of writing, they had other skills, such as metal work, weapon-making and agriculture, to a high degree. They had natural resources and they had space. An enforced colonization would enable the Romans to emerge out of the restrictions imposed by the narrow land of Italy, while at the same time extending the buffer zone between Rome and the dangerous tribes of Germany all the way along the Rhine. There is, therefore, some economic and social, as well as political, justification for Caesar's campaigns in Gaul.

THE CAMPAIGN OPENS 58 BC

The first people to show their hand were the Helvetti, who occupied the territory equivalent to modern Switzerland. They felt threatened not only by the Germanic tribes across the Rhine, but also by their neighbours in Gaul, the Aedui and the Sequani. As other civilizations had done in similar circumstances, they set out on a vast migration, aiming to settle on the west coast of Gaul.

KEY FACTS

The elected Celtic tribal chief could be a man or a woman. Immediately below the chief were two classes of landholders: the nobility (or knights), from whom the council of elders was drawn, and the wise men, comprising the priestly class (druids), the seers, and the bards. Some of those with special skills also had privileged status. Beneath the landless workers were the slaves, mainly debtors, prisoners-of-war, or bought from foreign slave traders.

The preferred route of the Helvetti took them through Transalpine Gaul. At Geneva, Caesar broke down their bridge over the Rhône and headed them off. The determined Helvetti now tried a more northern route, which took them through the territory of the Sequani and into that of the Aedui, who appealed for help from Rome. Caesar, delighted with a legitimate excuse for aggression, marched against them with his four legions, reinforced by two more which he had hastily recruited from non-Roman citizens of his province of Cisalpine Gaul. The battle of Bibracte, Caesar's first experience of a set-piece confrontation, was a triumph for tactical inspiration and Roman discipline.

Caesar drew up his army on the downward slope of a hill in the classic Roman formation of three lines, each eight men deep. His javelin fire was enough to disperse the massed ranks of Helvetti, who withdrew to a neighbouring hill slope and rallied their men. The Romans advanced against them in formation, only to be attacked on the left flank by 15,000 warriors of the tribes of Boii and Tulungi, who were part of the migration but had not so far been involved in the hostilities. Calmly, Caesar ordered his third line to about-turn, and then right-wheel to face this new threat, while his first two ranks still engaged the enemy. The result was total victory on both fronts.

The next trouble came from Ariovistus, chief of the Suebi, a Germanic tribe east of the Rhine. In return for aiding the Sequani against the Aedui, he had been dubbed by the senate a 'friend of Rome'. Now he was harassing the Aedui by settling members of his tribe rather too enthusiastically on land to which he was not fully entitled. The Aedui called on Caesar to remove him. Clearly this was a case first for trying diplomacy, but before that Caesar was called upon to put fire into the bellies of his army, some sectors of which were less than happy at the prospect of meeting the fearsome German hordes. He mustered all his centurions and, in a rousing harangue, announced that he was going to break camp during the final watch of the night: 'And even if no one else follows me, I shall march with the Tenth Legion alone.'

Caesar caught up with Ariovistus at Vesontio, where he made some pretence at negotiating a peaceful settlement. Neither side trusted the other. Ariovistus insisted that Caesar appear only with a cavalry escort, no legionaries. Caesar borrowed some horses from his Gallic auxiliary cavalry squadron and mounted on them crack infantrymen from the Tenth Legion. When the battle finally began, after six days of fencing and skirmishing, both sides charged at each other so fiercely that there was no time for the Romans to hurl their javelins. They just ran in with their swords. Caesar, on his own right wing, shattered the enemy opposite him. The Roman left wing was in trouble, but Publius Crassus, son of Marcus Crassus, who was in charge of the auxiliary cavalry, saw what was happening and ordered men from the third line of the right wing to reinforce their comrades on the left of the army. The threat from the Suebi was over, and those of their tribe who were massing on the eastern bank of the Rhine, waiting to cross, thought better of it, and went home.

Caesar had made an excellent start, so much so that he was able to cease hostilities before the end of the campaign season. He billeted his army for the winter among the friendly Sequani, with his legate, Titus Labienus in charge. He himself wintered in Cisalpine Gaul, where he could keep an eye on what was going on in Rome.

SECOND PHASE 57–54 BC

The mere presence of several legions in Gaul equipped for war was enough to alarm various tribes of the Belgae in the north, several of whom formed themselves into a federation, with the Nervii prominent among its ranks. While Caesar was performing a mopping-up operation on the Somme, the Belgae established themselves on the south bank of the river Sambre. Caesar was still making camp on the north bank, with his line of march, each legion followed by its baggage wagons, strung out across country, when the Belgae crossed the river in force, and attacked.

There was no time to form ranks. Each man simply rallied to the nearest standard. Those on the left of the haphazard line, mainly consisting of men of the Ninth and Tenth legions, stood firm, and then drove the opposition back across the river with great slaughter. The Nervii, however, under their chief Boduognatus, pushed back the Roman right, and were threatening to encircle it when Caesar arrived from supervising the legions on the left of the line. He seized a shield from a legionary and dashed to the front. There he ran up and down the line, steadying the ranks, and shouting encouragements to individual centurions by name.

The day was saved by the arrival of the two legions who had been bringing up the rear of the march, and by the ubiquitous Tenth Legion, whom Labienus ordered to disengage and join the battle on the Roman right. The fighting complement of the Nervii was wiped out. The older men of the tribe, hiding in the countryside with the women and children, surrendered to Caesar, who told them to go back to their homes and ordered neighbouring tribes not to molest them.

He was less generous to the Aduatuci. Their warriors had been on their way to back up the Nervii when they heard of the disaster. They returned home and, with their families and chattels, fortified themselves in a hill-top stronghold. Caesar invested the whole town with a fortified rampart. Then, under protective covering, a ramp and a siege tower were built. The people within the wall laughed, until they saw the tower moving towards them. Caesar offered to spare their lives, if they would give up all their arms. This they appeared to do, throwing them down from the top of the wall. It was only, however, a partial decommissioning. That night, several thousand armed Aduatuci broke out of the town and attacked the Roman camp. Most of them were killed; the rest retreated back through the gates. The next morning the Romans forced their way in. Caesar laconically described the fate of the inmates: 'Caesar sold off the whole town, lock, stock, and barrel. The dealers gave him a receipt for fifty-three thousand head of people' (*The Gallic War* II, 33). Slave dealers accompanied armies in ancient times, hoping to pick up their merchandise cheaply and in bulk. Sometimes, however, they got things spectacularly wrong, as in 165 BC, when they backed the Syrians to defeat the Maccabaean Jews.

Caesar spent the winter of 57–56 in Illyricum and Cisalpine Gaul. Though his despatches to the senate had earned in his honour an

> **KEY FACT**
>
> Caesar, who refers to himself throughout in the third person, wrote and published seven books (about 50,000 words) of *De Bello Gallico* in 51 BC. An eighth book, covering the events of 51 and 50, was added later by Aulus Hirtius, one of Caesar's officers.

unprecedented 15 days of public thanksgiving, he was far from satisfied with the impact he had been able to make on the global scene. Matters improved after a conference with Crassus and Pompey at Luca, where he was promised an extension of his command. This was confirmed by the senate in 55 under pressure, Crassus and Pompey having organized it that they would be consuls for that year.

Caesar's big thrust in 56 was against the western tribes in what is now Normandy and Brittany. The excuse was the behaviour of the Veneti. These maritime people, instead of meeting the Roman request for supplies of corn, had forcibly detained Caesar's envoys, demanding in exchange for their release the Venetian hostages who had been handed over as sureties for the tribe's good conduct. Neighbouring tribes followed suit. Caesar responded by building a fleet of warships on the

> **KEY FACT**
>
> Roman warships were rowed not by slaves, but by free men, who enlisted and served in the navy in the same way and under much the same conditions as their army colleagues.

Loire, and drafting in rowers and helmsmen from Transalpine Gaul. At first, however, the Roman ships could make little headway against the local vessels and their crews' local knowledge. Roman ingenuity prevailed, and Caesar's naval commander, Decimus Junius Brutus, devised an implement with sharp hooks mounted on a long pole, which cut the ropes supporting the yardarms and sails, causing them to collapse. The Venetian fleet was now at the mercy of the oar-driven Roman ships. A naval victory to Caesar! Having suffered the loss of all their ships and now their fighting men, the surviving male population surrendered to him. Caesar decided to make an example of them for detaining his envoys. He put to death all members of the council, and sold the rest to the slave dealers.

Trouble flared up in 55 on the other side of Gaul, where the restless Suebi had displaced other Germanic tribes, who had crossed the Rhine during the winter in search of places to settle. Caesar's march took him to the River Meuse, where protracted negotiations ensued with the representatives of the Germans. Both sides were guilty of sharp tactics. Caesar's 5,000 auxiliary cavalry, advancing under a banner of truce which had been agreed, were set upon and put to flight by 800 German horsemen. When the German leaders came to the Roman camp, as had been agreed, both to apologize for the behaviour of their cavalry and to extend the truce, Caesar ordered them to be held in chains. Then he led out his army in battle formation, with the cavalry at the rear to give them time to recover from the previous day's mauling.

He covered the 13 kilometres to the German camp before anyone there was aware of what was afoot. The survivors of the massacre, women and children among them, were pursued as far as the Rhine, where they were cut down or drowned.

As a final show of force, Caesar decided to cross the Rhine into enemy territory. He refused the offer of friendly tribesmen to ferry his army to the other side in river boats, as being beneath his dignity. Only the most spectacular method was good enough for Caesar! The Rhine at Coblenz is 400 metres wide, and six to eight metres deep. Caesar's engineers built a timber bridge right the way across, supported on massive piles driven into the stony bed of the river at an angle, so that the powerful current would not disturb them. According to Caesar himself, it was finished in ten days. A research team participated in a BBC television programme in 2000, in which conditions and methods were duplicated as far as possible, and concluded that, given the human skills and natural resources available to him, this was quite feasible.

Caesar now sent his army across into German territory where, for 18 days, they burned villages and buildings and cut down and destroyed crops. Then he returned across the bridge which, having served its purpose, was broken up.

CAESAR IN BRITAIN 55 AND 54 BC

Caesar's two landings in Britain may represent his most famous military exploits, but they are also his most inglorious. Various reasons have been suggested for these expeditions into the unknown. Caesar himself said that the Celts in Britain had been supporting the Celts on the mainland and needed teaching a lesson. Suetonius said he was after pearls, which, if this observation is true, must have proved a great disappointment, as British pearls were of poor quality. There was indeed very little of value to be obtained by way of booty, except slaves. It is more likely that Caesar feared being recalled by a senate which might regard him as having achieved his objectives in Gaul, and that a successful campaign would do him no harm in his rivalry with Pompey for public acclaim and support.

Though it was now late in the campaigning season, Caesar sent an officer to spy out the land and report back. This was done, though the man did not dare actually to disembark, for fear of what might happen to him in barbarian hands. Caesar decided to go ahead straight away with an exploratory expedition. He assembled the Seventh and Tenth legions at Boulogne and set sail during the night in the fleet that had done good service against the

Veneti, with the cavalry to cross separately in 18 transport ships. Because of bad weather, the cavalry was unable to disembark. Caesar sailed eastwards along the coast, looking for somewhere to land his infantry, while on shore tribesmen tracked the fleet, hurling missiles and abuse from the cliffs.

Caesar decided to disembark his army on the shore by Deal, but because it was low tide his ships could not get in close enough. Instead his soldiers had to drop down into the water and wade to the beach, loaded down with their personal kit, in the face of a concentration of enemy missiles and cavalry assaults.

There was a general reluctance to proceed, until the *aquilifer* of the Tenth shouted out to his colleagues: 'Jump, men, if you don't want to lose the eagle to the enemy: at least they'll say of me that I did my duty to country and my general!' With that, he launched himself into the water and waded towards the enemy, carrying the eagle in front of him. The troops, mumbling among themselves about not wishing to be disgraced, followed him.

The brief campaign was a case of win some, lose some. Owing to the weather Caesar was still without his cavalry, which would normally have been essential to combat the fast British chariots, each manned by a driver and a warrior. He still defeated the opposing force, and took the statutory hostages. He also saw off a British attack on the Seventh, whose men were out in the corn-fields foraging for supplies. He was lucky, however, to get his army back across the Channel at all. He totally misjudged the tides and the weather, and as a result the ships which he had drawn up on the shore were flooded, and the transports lying out at anchor were subjected to fierce gales. Several ships broke up and others were too damaged to sail. Caesar crammed his soldiers into the ships which had survived and withdrew for the winter.

Before leaving for his province in Italy, Caesar ordered a new invasion fleet of 600 transports and 28 galleys to be built to his specifications.

They would be lower in the water and shallower in the draught, for ease of beaching and unloading, and the transports would be fitted with oars as well as sails.

He was all ready to embark in the spring of 54, when trouble blew up in Gaul. Dumnorix, of the Aedui, had persuaded several other chiefs to join him in an armed revolt. The powerful Treveri, who never attended Caesar's council meetings of tribal representatives, were even actively negotiating with German tribes across the Rhine. Caesar took four legions and 800 cavalry and force-marched them into the territory of the Treveri. The solution, however, was one of diplomacy rather than arms. There were two opposing factions within the Treveri, led respectively by Cingetorix and Indutiomarus. Cingetorix took the initiative by pledging his loyalties to Rome. Caesar then rebuffed the claims of friendship by Indutiomarus and ordered him to hand over 200 hostages, including his son and the rest of his family.

When he got back to Boulogne, Caesar sent out orders for all the tribal chiefs of Gaul to meet him there. Those that arrived who he thought might be antagonistic to Rome, he immediately detained, to be kept under his personal supervision on the expedition to Britain, so that they could not make trouble in his absence. Dumnorix pleaded to be excused, on the grounds that he was a bad sailor. When Caesar refused to release him, he escaped, but was hunted down and killed.

The huge invasion fleet crossed the Channel in July 54. To save time, Caesar anchored the ships that would remain with him off the unprotected shore, rather than drag them up the beach. The rest he sent back empty to Gaul. Then he marched inland to find the opposition. Two days later he received the news that his British fleet had been wrecked again. The damage was catastrophic. Some ships had dragged their anchors in the storm, or snapped their cables, and had been bodily thrown up on the beach. Others had crashed against each other in the water and had broken up. Caesar returned to the scene and ordered the rebuilding of those ships which were not damaged beyond repair. To do this he withdrew craftsmen from his legions and obtained ships' carpenters from Gaul. He also wrote to Labienus in Gaul to have as many new ships as possible built by the army. Then he started out again.

The Britons were ready for him. As leader, they had elected Cassivellaunus, chief of the Catuvellauni, from north of the Thames. For a time his guerrilla tactics succeeded, but it was inevitable that he had to make a stand somewhere. At the same time, in an attempt to cause a diversion and also paralyse Caesar's lines of communication, Cassivellaunus sent orders to the maritime tribes in Kent to carry out an attack on the Roman naval camp. This was repulsed by the ten cohorts and 300 cavalary which Caesar had left there to guard the ships.

Cassivellaunus took up a position fortified with stakes on the far bank of the Thames, at a point where it could just be forded. Caesar sent his cavalry in first, followed by the legions, up to their necks in the water. So fierce was the assault, however, that the Britons abandoned their positions and retreated into the woody countryside. Caesar marched eastwards, into the land of the Trinobantes, whom he induced to surrender to him, thus depriving Cassivellaunus of a powerful ally. Cassivellaunus, who was no fool, capitulated rather than endure a long war of attrition. This also suited Caesar, who had had disturbing reports of 'sudden commotions' in Gaul, and was anxious to return there for the winter.

Caesar fixed an annual rate of tribute which the British tribes should pay to Rome, of which probably only the first instalment was delivered, and requisitioned a large number of hostages and prisoners. At the coast, the refurbished ships were lying ready. Even with the 60 new ships which Labienus had prepared, and the original ones which had returned to Gaul, it would still be necesary for each ship to make two trips. In the end, because of the weather, only a few of the ships from Gaul reached Britain; the rest were driven back by the wind and the tide. Caesar packed his transports tighter than he had intended, and brought his army and his human booty safely across. In two campaigns he had achieved nothing tangible. It would be 97 years before the crested helmets of the legions were seen again in Britain.

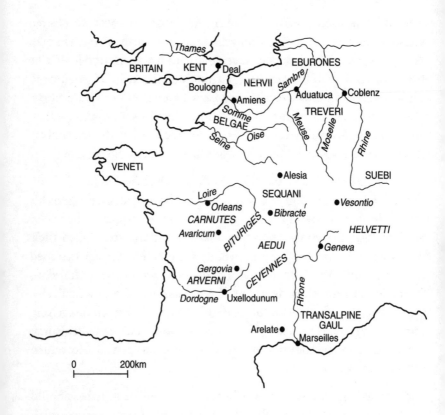

Map 3 Gaul

REVOLT IN GAUL 53–51 BC

The 'sudden commotions' which had made Caesar's return to Gaul imperative, exploded into a bloodbath. Ambiorix, chief of the Eburones, while professing friendship to Rome, inveigled the newly raised legion holding the camp at Aduatuca into abandoning it for reasons of safety, to join up with the legion nearest them. The latter was commanded by Quintus Cicero, brother of Marcus. The column was ambushed and massacred on the way.

Ambiorix now encouraged the Nervii to take a leaf out of Caesar's book and besiege Cicero, which they did so effectively that Cicero was forced to ask for Caesar's help. Caesar was at Amiens. He left immediately, but with far fewer troops than he would have liked. The Nervii broke off the siege and surged along the way to meet him. Outnumbered by ten to one, Caesar constructed a camp deliberately smaller than would normally be the case, in order to deceive the opposition as to his numbers. Then he ordered his men to feign panic. The Nervii gathered round, scenting easy victory. A single sally, from all the gates at once, was enough to put them to flight. Caesar was just in time. When Cicero's men were paraded for him, nine-tenths of them were walking wounded.

While various groupings of hostile tribes were taking place, Caesar raised two extra legions from Cisalpine Gaul, and borrowed a third from Pompey. He held conferences of Gallic chiefs, and took punitive action against those who failed to turn up. He neatly avoided committing his legionaries to fighting the Eburones in the unfavourable forests, by inviting neighbouring tribes to join him in pillaging their lands. Ambiorix escaped, but Caesar took his revenge out on Acco, chief of the Senones, who had incited his tribe not to co-operate with the Romans. At the next meeting of the chiefs, he was flogged to death.

While Caesar was taking his habitual winter sojourn in his province, observing from a distance events in Rome, there emerged a new resolve on the part of the insurgents, and a new threat. The Carnutes struck at the heart of Caesar's lines of supply, and also at Roman protocol, by massacring Roman merchants who had made a commercial base at Orleans, a significant centre of the corn trade. At the same time, the confederacy of hostile tribes found a charismatic leader in Vercingetorix, chief of the Arverni.

The main body of Caesar's army was disposed in various parts of northeastern Gaul. He had with him in Italy only a force of new recruits and a supplementary levy from his province. He decided to march with these, rather than risk summoning his regular troops, who might on the way have to fight a battle without him. Vercingetorix was among the Bituriges, inciting them to join his cause, when Caesar suddenly irrupted into Arvernian territory across the Cevennes, through passes which at that time of year were two metres deep in snow. It was a feint. While Vercingetorix hurried back home, Caesar marched his rudimentary force towards the Seine, where he had ordered his army to concentrate. Then he recrossed the Loire to attack Avaricum, the heavily fortified settlement of the Bituriges.

The tactics of Vercingetorix were to hover around the Romans to prevent food supplies getting through to them. With no chance of starving out the people of Avaricum, Caesar resorted to siege engines, and constructed a ramp up to the top of the wall. The people inside retaliated by hurling down balls of lighted pitch to set the apparatus alight, and digging a tunnel underneath it to create more havoc. Caesar brought up his dart-throwing catapults, but whenever a Gaul on the walls was shot, another took his place. Even with food running out, Caesar's soldiers insisted on maintaining the attack, rather than lose the chance of taking revenge for the murder of the Roman merchants. It was finally successful. Of the 40,000 inhabitants, less than 800 escaped the inevitable slaughter that followed; these had leapt from the walls as the final assault began, and made their way to Vercingetorix.

Next on Caesar's list was Gergovia, in the territory of the Arverni. Caesar's subterfuge there failed, due to the indiscipline of part of his army. The result was a defeat for Rome. Caesar had made up the baggage mules, with their handlers wearing military helmets in the saddle, to look like cavalry, and sent them towards one part of the town, while at the other end a legion of infantry was to obliterate the camp Vercingetorix had established, and then retire. The soldiers ignored the instructions to retreat, and were repulsed with the loss of 46 centurions

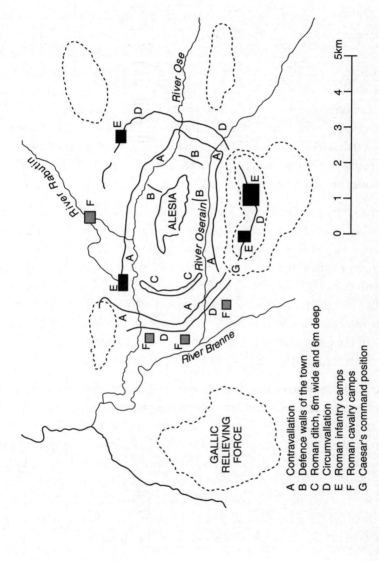

Map 4 The siege of Alesia

A Contravallation
B Defence walls of the town
C Roman ditch, 6m wide and 6m deep
D Circumvallation
E Roman infantry camps
F Roman cavalry camps
G Caesar's command position

and 700 legionaries. The next day Caesar assembled his troops and gave them a lecture on military tactics and the importance of obeying orders.

So far Vercingetorix had got many things right, against a master strategist. Also, of all the tribes in Gaul, only three still supported Caesar. At this point, however, Vercingetorix made his first and, as it turned out, his last tactical error. He withdrew, with his cavalry and about 80,000 infantry, to the stronghold of Alesia, which stood on a plateau bounded on three sides by rivers. Caesar established a blockade of the town, which he surrounded with an elaborate series of ditches and earthworks (contravallation). To protect himself from attacks by a relieving force, he then constructed a further ring of fortifications outside the first (circumvallation).

Vercingetorix made several sorties out of the gates, but his men were severely mauled by Caesar's German cavalry. To save food, and also to summon assistance, Vercingetorix managed to get his cavalry out of the town by night, with instructions to raise the tribes. Both sides were now running short of supplies. One of Vercingetorix's lieutenants advocated killing the elderly citizens of the town and eating them. A compromise was reached. All civilians, with their wives and children, were turned out of the gates. Caesar posted sentries on the ramparts and refused to let them through, leaving them to starve in no-man's-land.

The Gallic relieving force duly arrived and encamped on the heights to the west of the town. It was enormous, comprising some 250,000 infantry alone, against Caesar's estimated 70,000 troops. There were two battles, one by day and the other by night. Caesar, conspicuous in his red cloak, was forced to fight on two fronts. While the Gauls assailed the Roman outer line of defences at various points, Vercingetorix with his warriors made sallies out of the town against the inner line. Caesar himself led the final *coup de main*, appearing with four cohorts and a troop of cavalry to reinforce an attack on the Gallic rear.

There was slaughter and wholesale surrender. Vercingetorix was sent to Rome in chains. Caesar spared members of the Aedui and the Arverni, to make it easier to recover their territories for Rome. The rest of the prisoners were distributed as booty to the Roman troops, one per man.

Alesia marked the end of concerted Gallic resistance, but not quite the end of hostilities. Pockets of resistance had to be mopped up. For this reason, Caesar wintered in Bibracte with a 30-year-old officer called Mark Antony as his quartermaster-general. He left Antony in charge early in 51, while he went to sort out the Bituriges. On this occasion he showed great clemency, in order to demonstrate that it was better to be friends with Rome, than to be her enemies.

No such treatment was afforded to the rebels at Uxellodunum, who holed themselves up with enough supplies to last some time. When Caesar arrived, the siege was under way. He summed up the position and instructed his engineers as to how to cut off the town's water supply. The inhabitants capitulated. Caesar had the hands of all those who had borne arms amputated, to discourage others from continuing the struggle.

Caesar had achieved in Gaul a sort of peace, on his own terms, and had added to the Roman empire a territory twice the size of Italy, with a population far greater than that of Spain. Now it was time to attend to his more personal affairs and to other matters affecting his career development.

MEANWHILE, BACK IN ROME 58–51 BC
It is a matter for conjecture whether the year of power Clodius was enabled to exercise in 58 gave notice of the havoc one man could cause to the constitution, or of the need to have a single person at the helm of state who could control excessive behaviour. His legislation largely reduced the administration to chaos, especially his crowd-pleasing measure to substitute free corn for supplies at reduced prices for those in need. His gangs of thugs, established under the cover of craftsmen's

guilds, roamed the streets, making trouble. He even set them on Pompey, who was forced to barricade himself in his villa outside the city walls. Pompey retaliated by forming his own private army of urban guerrillas, under the command of Titus Annius Milo, a rich aristocrat who had held public office, and was popular with the mob for his provision of public entertainments.

When Clodius's term of office ended, there was nothing to obstruct the introduction of a law calling for Cicero's return from exile. Pompey used his influence to enable it to have a smooth passage through the senate, as well as his gang of hoodlums to ensure that there was no opposition from supporters of Clodius when it came before the popular assembly. Cicero returned the compliment by proposing, two days after his return in 57, that Pompey should be appointed corn-supply supremo. Pompey undertook this office with admirable efficiency; it also kept him in the public eye.

There was now a setback to the smooth progress of the plans of the triumvirate of Caesar, Crassus, and Pompey. Lucius Domitius Ahenobarbus, brother-in-law and a staunch supporter of Cato, who was due to return to Rome in 55, announced that he was standing as a candidate for the consulship in 55, and that if elected he would press for Caesar to be recalled from Gaul immediately to face whatever music his enemies had in store for him.

This was the background to the emergency meeting of the triumvirate at Luca. Crassus and Pompey returned to Rome to take part in the consular elections. That they were successful over Ahenobarbus was due to terror tactics on the part of Pompey's gangs and Caesar's neat ploy of sending on leave to Rome enough of his soldiers to tip the electoral balance.

During their term as consuls, Crassus and Pompey filled as many of the public appointments as they could with their own supporters, through whose offices they obtained official sanction for the extension of Caesar's command until 50, and for themselves until then the plum jobs of the governorship of Syria for Crassus, and of Spain for Pompey. Pompey used his job on the corn supply as a pretext to exercise his governorship from Rome, where he could continue to exert political influence.

In 54 the personal link between Caesar and Pompey was broken, when Julia died in childbirth, together with the child she was carrying. Caesar suggested that he might now divorce Calpurnia and marry Pompey's daughter, and that Pompey might marry Octavia, Caesar's great-niece, the granddaughter of his sister Julia (minor). Pompey would have none of this. Instead, he married Cornelia, of the influential family of Metellus, who was the widow of a son of Crassus.

Meanwhile, Crassus was energetically enriching himself in Syria. He denuded the great Temple in Jerusalem of its treasures, and then embarked on a misguided attempt to acquire military laurels by taking on the Parthians. He was ignominiously defeated, and then murdered while attempting to negotiate the terms of his surrender. It is said that the Parthians cut off his head, and poured molten gold into his mouth, as a symbol of Crassus's greed.

In Rome, widescale political bribery brought government to a halt, as the tribunes of the people used their vetoes to block anything constructive. Total anarchy reigned in 52 after Clodius was killed in a clash between his gang and Milo's. There were riots, and the senate-house and other buildings in the Forum were burned down. Pompey, conveniently on the spot, was appointed sole consul with effectively the powers of a dictator, to calm things down. He did so firmly and efficiently, bringing in several significant measures. There must now be

KEY FACT

As marriage in Rome was based on consent, the consent of either party was all that was required for divorce. The wife's father also counted as a consenting party. Cato was involved in a bizarre case. He was asked by the orator Hortensius to dissolve his daughter's marriage to Bibulus so that Hortensius could marry her himself. Cato refused. Hortensius then persuaded Cato to divorce his own wife, Marcia, whom Hortensius then married. When Hortensius died in 50 BC, leaving Marcia a rich widow, Cato remarried her.

a five-year gap between a consul proceeding to a provincial governorship. The convention that no one could stand for office in their absence was reaffirmed. This did not, however, apply to Caesar, on whose behalf Pompey had previously obtained a ruling that at the end of his command he could stand as consul for 48 without leaving Gaul.

DECISIONS, DECISIONS

Caesar spent some months in 51 writing up his campaign notes for publication. He also had to work out what he would do after his next term as consul expired, since now he could not immediately get a further command. There were also renewed problems for him in Rome. The consuls for the year 50 demanded his return, on the grounds that the war, in pursuit of which Caesar had requested an extension of his contract, was over. Caesar managed to bribe one of them and also, by the same means, got over to his side Gaius Scribonius Curio. Curio, a bosom pal of Mark Antony in their youth, now a tribune of the people, had been causing all sorts of difficulties for Caesar's supporters. Now, he simply vetoed any proposed legislation that was not in Caesar's interests.

Caesar moved one of his legions from Gaul to his province in north Italy, claiming that it was needed there in case of trouble in Illyricum. His overall manpower was neutralized, however, by a neat piece of tactical legerdemain on the part of Pompey. More troops were needed in the east, against the Parthians. Pompey declared that he would release one of his legions in Spain, if Caesar would give up one of his. When Caesar agreed, Pompey nominated as his contribution the legion Caesar had borrowed from him in 53. Caesar thus lost two legions. He also lost the initiative, for when the two legions arrived in Italy it was decided that the Parthian situation had improved, and they were put at the disposal of Pompey.

The situation was boiling up into a confrontation between Caesar and Pompey which could easily develop into civil war. There were several attempts on both sides to arrive at a compromise. Caesar was finally ordered to lay down his command. He replied that he would only do so if Pompey did the same. The senate broke the deadlock by declaring a state of emergency.

The River Rubicon, by an administrative accident, was the northern limit of the environs of the town of Ariminum (now Rimini). It was also the boundary between the province of Cisalpine Gaul and Italy. By law, Caesar could not leave his province without losing his command; by bringing armed soldiers into Italy he became an enemy of the state. He ordered his men to go on ahead, while he set out from Ravenna in a closed carriage by a different route. Just before dawn on 11 January 49, he arrived at the north bank of the river. Here it is said that he paused in thought, before pronouncing, 'Alea jacta est,' and crossing the Rubicon by the little bridge to the other side.

KEY FACT

Alea jacta est, 'The die is cast' (more literally, 'The dice has been thrown') has as its modern equivalent in the croupier's cry of 'Rien ne va plus'. In Roman times, gambling with dice was strictly only allowed during the feast of Saturnalia in December. Of the two kinds of dice, the tessera was a cube exactly like the modern version, with the figures 1 to 6 on its sides. Three dice were shaken in a vessel, and then thrown onto the board or the floor. The best possible throw was three sixes.

5 Caesar – The Dictator 49–45 BC

Caesar could not stand any longer someone above him,
Nor could Pompey abide anyone being his equal.

Lucan, *The Civil War* I, 125–6

When news of Caesar's incursion into Italy reached Rome, the senate acted calmly and prudently. Successors were appointed to Caesar's governorships in the provinces. War was declared against him and Pompey was entrusted with the defence of the state and the command of its armed forces.

It was to be a one-sided war, but it had to be fought on several fronts. Caesar had with him the Thirteenth Legion, formed in 57, and eight further legions in Gaul, two of which were on the march to join him. His track record as a military strategist was supreme, and his soldiers were with him to a man, especially when it was revealed that he had doubled their basic rate of pay. Though now in his 51st year, he was, apart from his mild epilepsy, a fit man, hardened by ten years' campaigning. Pompey was now 56, at a time when many males, if they survived childhood, died in their twenties or thirties. He had seen no active service since 62, and he had in 50 been incapacitated by what would appear to be a stomach ulcer. He had seven legions in Spain, as well as the two in Italy, plus a fleet of 500 warships and numerous galleys, some of which were positioned in strategic ports around the Mediterranean.

CIVIL WAR – FIRST PHASE, ITALY AND SPAIN 49 BC

Caesar had experienced lieutenants, including Mark Antony. Labienus, however, defected to the other side. Caesar cheekily sent on after him his possessions and cash. He then seized the initiative from Pompey by advancing down the main east-coast road and from there making strikes against crucial towns inland which commanded the northern route to Rome. When, three weeks later, units of the Thirteenth reassembled at Ancona, Caesar also had garrisons in Pisaurum, Fanum, Arretium and Iguvium.

Meanwhile, there was consternation in Rome. Those outside the city came rushing in, and those inside hastily made their departure. Pompey ordered the evacuation of the city and went to Capua, where he instructed the senate and consuls to reconvene. Caesar's advance became inexorable. The crucial crossroads' town of Corfinium, held for Pompey by Ahenobarbus, capitulated, with the three legions Ahenobarbus had personally raised. Men flocked to join Caesar, or allowed themselves to be pressed into his service. In all he enrolled 16 new legions at this time, some of which had originally been intended for Pompey's camp.

Pompey withdrew to Brundisium with his two legions of veterans and whatever other troops he could find, with the intention of embarking with them for Greece, and there to regroup his forces. Caesar followed him, sending messages ahead asking for talks. Pompey ignored them. By the time Caesar arrived, Pompey had got half his army away, while the other half waited for the transports to return. Caesar besieged the town, but was unable to prevent the second embarkation. Leaving his exhausted troops in Apulia, Caesar then travelled to Rome, which he had not seen for nine years. He selected the praetor Marcus Aemilius Lepidus to reconvene the few senators left in the city, and attempted to form some sort of central administration. When the senators refused to vote him any funds to prosecute the war, he broke into the public treasury and took them for himself.

Caesar then put Lepidus in charge of the city and, leaving Antony to look after the rest of Italy, marched with six legions for Spain, to secure himself from having a potentially dangerous army at his back when he took the war to Pompey. He also sent Curio to Africa with three legions, where the sitting governor had come out in favour of Pompey.

There was a further trouble-maker in Juba, king of Numidia, whose beard Caesar had tweaked during an altercation some 13 years earlier. Curio was too inexperienced for such a mission, and lost his life and two of his legions in an ambush. His head, which was cut off and taken to Juba.

The campaign in Spain, against well-drilled Roman legions under two capable commanders, was decided in 40 days, virtually without bloodshed. Caesar outmanoeuvred his opponents at Ilerda by a combination of skilled engineering (bridge-building and the construction of a ford), ingenuity (building coracles, such as he had seen in Britain, as transports), and surprise forced marches, while all the time facing serious supply problems. After the surrender of the Pompey force, there was some fraternization between the two sides. One of Pompey's commanders gave orders that any of Caesar's men found in his camp would be executed. Caesar responded by ordering that any Pompey supporter harboured by his men should be well treated and sent back to his own lines. A number of Pompey's military tribunes and centurions opted to stay with Caesar, who enlisted them in his army and allowed them to retain their ranks.

Caesar left several legions in Spain, to prevent trouble, and sent the rest ahead of him into Italy. He returned via Corduba, where he had called a meeting of representatives of all communities in Spain, and Cadiz, from which he took a ship to Tarraco. In September he reached Marseilles, where he received the news that Lepidus had advised the senate to appoint him dictator. He had to leave in a hurry, however, for Placentia, where there was a potential mutiny of his troops. They were complaining that they had not had the bonus which he promised them while they were in Brundisium. The trouble had begun with the Ninth Legion. He announced that he had no alternative but to carry out the punishment of decimation. This would have involved losing about 500 valuable men. Pretending to show mercy, he instead had the 120 ringleaders picked out, and condemned 12 of them to death. One of them proved that he had an alibi for when the mutiny began. Caesar pardoned him and executed instead the centurion who had accused the man.

When he reached Rome, Caesar formally accepted the office of dictator and embarked on a frenzied round of political activity. As presiding officer, he held elections for the consulship for the following year. He himself stood as a candidate and duly announced himself elected with, as his consular colleague, Publius Servilius Isauricus, under whose father he had served briefly in the east in 78. Eleven days after arriving in Rome, Caesar abdicated as dictator and set off for Brundisium, where he had ordered his army to muster, ready to embark for Greece.

CIVIL WAR – SECOND PHASE, GREECE 48 BC

Caesar stole a march on Pompey by crossing during the winter, normally a closed season for maritime operations. There were not enough ships to carry the whole of his army, even close-packed together and carrying a minimum of personal baggage. He sailed with half his men, including several legions which had just marched from northern Spain, and landed them on the coast of Epirus before Bibulus, lying off Corfu with 100 ships of Pompey's fleet, woke up to what was happening. Bibulus managed to catch 30 of the transports on their way back to Brundisium, and was in such a rage at his own incompetence that he set fire to them and burned their crews alive.

Antony, in Italy with the rest of the army and the stragglers who had arrived late, now had to contend not only with the weather but also with the close attentions of Pompey's fleet. At one point Caesar got so frustrated by the delay that he determined to fetch the troops himself. Disguised in a full cloak, he infiltrated himself onto a small boat and ordered the captain, in Caesar's name, to set sail. As soon as they got out into the open sea a gale blew up and the captain instructed the helmsman to turn about. Whereupon Caesar revealed himself. 'Come on now,' he shouted, as though this would solve all their problems, 'You're carrying Caesar and all his hopes!' The elements took no notice and, in spite of the efforts of the oarsmen, the boat was forced to return to shore.

The next part of the campaign developed into a game of cat and mouse. Antony finally managed to bring across the rest of the troops, intending to join up with Caesar at Apollonia. Instead, because of the prevailing wind, he landed to the north of Dyrrachium, where Pompey had concentrated his forces. Caesar attempted to besiege Pompey into submission, but Pompey could receive supplies by sea, and it was Caesar who ran short of food. Pompey was able to break out after, according to Caesar himself, six battles had taken place in the course of a single day. Pompey used his Cretan archers to devastating effect. When it was all over, the men in one of Caesar's defensive outworks picked up 30,000 arrows which had been fired at them. Four centurions in one cohort lost an eye. The shield of another centurion had 120 arrow holes in it, and its owner was still alive. Caesar presented him with a generous bonus and promoted him to *pilus primus*.

Caesar disengaged his troops and led them into the plains of Thessaly, where the rich cornfields would provide supplies of food. The wounded he billeted in Apollonia. Pompey's chief dilemma was whether to embark his army for Italy, leaving Caesar, who had no command of the sea and no ships, the uphill task of marching his army back to Italy to defend it, or whether to go after him and, as it were, kill two birds with one stone. He was persuaded by the aristocrats in his entourage to do battle.

The two sides met near Pharsalus. Pompey had the advantage of numbers. His tactics were to maintain pressure on Caesar's infantry all along the line, and then outflank Caesar's right with a massed cavalry attack. Caesar combated this ploy by removing one cohort from each of his legions' third line, and redeploying them in reserve behind his right wing. At the critical moment these men took up the offensive, using their javelins against the cavalry as bayonets. The Pompeian cavalry, caught by surprise, interfered with each other, and took flight. Seeing this, Caesar threw his third line, which had not yet engaged the enemy, into the assault. Pompey's infantry could not sustain the fight and fled from the field. At this, Pompey himself completely lost his nerve and galloped into the distance. Six thousand of his soldiers were dead. Twenty-four thousand more surrendered to Caesar, who added them to his complement of troops, with instructions that none of them should be victimized. Among the senior officers to whom he gave immunity was Marcus Junius Brutus, the son of his mistress Servilia.

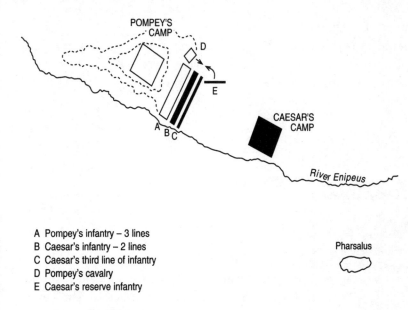

A Pompey's infantry – 3 lines
B Caesar's infantry – 2 lines
C Caesar's third line of infantry
D Pompey's cavalry
E Caesar's reserve infantry

Map 5 The Battle of Pharsalus

INTERLUDE IN EGYPT 48–47 BC

Caesar now had much the same problem as had faced Pompey. He could have returned to Italy in triumph. He could have mopped up the Pompeians who had escaped from Pharsalus. These fugitives were even now making arrangements to regroup in force in Africa. Instead, following his private agenda and personal vendetta, Caesar set out to track down Pompey.

He sent Antony back to Italy to look after his interests there. This Antony did very effectively, for the senate appointed Caesar dictator for the whole of the succeeding year, with Antony as his *magister equitum*. Caesar made Gnaius Domitius Calvinus, a former consul and Pompey supporter who had defected to Caesar's camp, governor of Asia, and gave him three of Pompey's legions. Pompey himself had sailed to Mytilene, on the island of Lesbos, to pick up his wife, who had been staying there during the hostilities. He was next heard of in Cyprus. Caesar guessed he was heading for Egypt and set out in pursuit, with two under-strength legions, a squadron of cavalry and an escort of ten warships.

KEY FACT

Marcus Junius Brutus (85–42 BC) was largely brought up by Cato, his mother's half-brother, after his father's death when he was eight. He later married Cato's daughter, Porcia. He was involved in a money-lending scandal, when his syndicate lent a large sum of money to the people of Salamis at 48 per cent interest, four times the legal maximum. When the debt was not repaid, they locked up the town council in the municipal hall until some of them starved to death. Caesar appointed Brutus governor of Cisalpine Gaul in 46, and a praetor in 44.

KEY FACT

The statutory term of office for a dictator was six months only. By a tradition going back to the establishment of the republic in 509 BC, the dictator was also *magister populi* (commander-in-chief, infantry). He nominated his deputy, *magister equitum* (commander-in-chief, cavalry).

The Egyptian political situation at the time was mind-boggling, even by the standards of the ancient world. Egypt was ruled by the Hellenistic dynasty of the Ptolemies, founded by one of Alexander's generals. The country had been bequeathed to Rome in 81 BC, since when its rulers had maintained its independence by paying bribes to the senate. Ptolemy XII Auletes paid further sums to the triumvirate of Caesar, Crassus, and Pompey, in order to be recognized as the rightful ruler, which he was not. On his death in 51, Auletes left his kingdom jointly to his daughter, Cleopatra VII (68–30 BC) and his son, Ptolemy XIII (61–47 BC), adjuring the Roman people to ensure that the provisions of his will were carried out.

In accordance with the protocol that monarchs were living gods and could not marry mortals, Cleopatra married her brother. He, as a minor, was advised by his chief ministers. Neither Cleopatra nor Ptolemy, however, wished to share the throne with anyone else. Their two armies fought each other. Cleopatra was defeated and took refuge in Syria, where she raised another army. Now she was back, encamped outside Alexandria.

Pompey's ship arrived in the great harbour of Alexandria in September 48. He sent a message to Ptolemy asking for asylum. Ptolemy's advisers decided that it was better to have Pompey out of the way altogether. They lured him ashore, where he was stabbed in the back, while his wife could only look on.

KEY FACT

Egypt submitted to Alexander without a fight in 332 BC, and he ordered the city of Alexandria, which became the capital, to be founded in his honour. At his unexpected death in 323, no one commanded sufficient power to succeed to his vast empire, which ultimately devolved on three of his generals, Antigonus, the 'one-eyed', Ptolemy, and Seleucus.

A few days later, Caesar sailed in to Alexandria, to be presented with Pompey's embalmed head, from which he recoiled in horror. He accepted Pompey's signet ring, however, and is said to have wept over it. Shortly afterwards, he received a visitor.

Cleopatra arrived in a sack for storing bedclothes, carried over the shoulder of a male attendant. He untied it in Caesar's presence, and the queen emerged. The ostensible purpose of her visit was to get Caesar to arbitrate in the dispute with her brother. It was not a fair adjudication. Whether she was a sex-kitten, or just exotic and available, has been argued ever since. The poet Lucan, writing only a few generations later, was in little doubt:

> Vain would have been her address
>   To the obdurate ears of a jury.
> Judged on her looks, not her case,
>   With come-hither eyes as her counsel,

> Passionately she appealed,
> And a passionate night was the outcome.
>
> Lucan, *The Civil War* X, 105–6

Caesar, besotted, now got himself involved in a local war. Achillas, commander of the young king's army, who resented Caesar's interference as well as his favouritism, brought up forces and besieged the palace, which backed onto the harbour. With Caesar were Cleopatra and Ptolemy XIII, and their younger siblings, Arsinoe and another Ptolemy. Riots broke out in the town and many of Caesar's soldiers were killed. With the small force remaining to him he fortified the palace environs, and he had access to the harbour. He sent out frantic calls for reinforcements, both of men and ships. His first thought was to destroy the Egyptian fleet; in the resulting conflagration the 250-year-old library was partially destroyed. Several battles took place in and around the harbour, notably for possession of the causeway joining the island of Pharos, with its famous lighthouse, to the mainland. In the course of one of these scraps, Caesar found himself in the undignified position of having to jump into the sea and swim to safety. This he did with ease, throwing off his heavy outer garments in the water and, it is said, at the same time holding out of the water in his left hand a number of valuable documents to keep them dry.

Arsinoe, wishing perhaps to have a share in the action if not of her sister's elderly lover, slipped out of the palace with her eunuch, Ganymedes, and joined up with Achillas. There was an argument. Achillas was assassinated, and Ganymedes emerged as his successor. Ganymedes now hatched a devilish scheme to replace the fresh water that ran through conduits to the palace area with sea water, which he introduced into the system by means of water-wheels. Caesar countered this ploy by ordering wells to be dug in the palace grounds.

It was possibly to rid himself of another source of trouble that Caesar bowed to envoys from outside, and allowed them to take Ptolemy XIII back to his supporters. To have a figurehead, not to say also a godhead, among them, galvanized the Egyptian army to renewed efforts.

Caesar was finally extricated from his embarrassing military situation the following spring by troops collected from Cilicia and Syria, together with a Jewish army under Antipater, a wealthy Idumaean power-broker. This ad hoc force entered Egypt by way of Ashkelon and occupied Pelusium. Caesar broke out of the palace environs, his troops now bolstered by the arrival of one of Domitius's legions and of the Twenty-Seventh Legion, which he had ordered to follow him from Pharsalus. The Egyptians were trapped between

KEY FACTS

As a reward for his services, Caesar appointed Antipater (d. 43 BC) procurator (admini-strator) of Judaea. He also subsequently passed measures to protect the interests of Jews outside Judaea. Antipater's younger son became Herod the Great, king of Judaea 37–4 BC.

the two forces in the delta of the Nile. Ptolemy drowned, and Arsinoe was captured and sent to Rome. Cleopatra's 11-year-old younger brother became Ptolemy XIV, and also her new husband. The son she had later in the year, however, was Caesar's: he became known as Caesarion.

There was time for the unmarried couple to have a two-month honeymoon on the Nile before Caesar said his goodbyes. As a going-away present, he gave Cleopatra Cyprus, and left with her some troops that he could ill afford to spare. He set out at the head of a very depleted Sixth Legion to make the long march back to Rome. On the way he intended to see what could be done about Pharnaces, king of Pontus and son of Mithridates, who had overrun Cappadocia and part of Armenia, massacring, mutilating, or imprisoning every Roman citizen that he found.

VENI, VIDI, VICI

The battle of Zela in August 47 is one of the more extraordinary in the history of the ancient world. Caesar had two legions, the faithful Sixth and the Thirty-Seventh, another loan on the part of Domitius. He also had a Roman-style legion raised and trained locally by the king of lower Armenia, and some Asian auxiliaries which he had collected en route.

Zela is in the mountains. In defiance of the gloomy predictions of his augurs, Caesar took possession, by night, of the summit of a hill opposite the enemy camp, and separated from it by a ravine. There he began to dig fortifications. At dawn Pharnaces drew up his army in front of his camp, and then launched a surprise uphill assault on the Roman position from the ravine. An astonished Caesar ordered his men to exchange their trenching tools for their weapons and to form up in defensive array. They forced the enemy back into the ravine, and there slaughtered them. It was of this encounter that Caesar coined the aphorism, '*Veni, vidi, vici*' ('I came, I saw, I conquered').

Caesar now tidied up military and political affairs in the region, and returned to Italy by sea. He landed at Tarentum in late September or early October 47. From there, he went overland to Brundisium, where an anxious Cicero was to meet him. At the onset of civil war, Cicero had backed the wrong side. Though he was not at the battle of Pharsalus, he was in Greece at the time. After it, he had nowhere to go except back to Italy. He landed at Brundisium, but got no farther. A message came from Antony, who hated Cicero for his treatment of Lentulus, Antony's stepfather, over the Catiline affair. Caesar had given orders in writing that no supporter of Pompey's cause was to be allowed back into Italy without his express permission. Until Caesar returned to Italy and ruled on his case, Cicero must remain where he was.

Cicero waited for Caesar just outside the town gates, with other local dignitaries behind him. When Caesar saw him, he jumped down from his horse and hugged him. They then had a private conversation, the upshot of which seems to have been that Cicero was free to go where he liked.

KEY FACTS

Caesar had no reason to like Cicero, but he admired his professionalism as a speaker and writer. He dedicated to Cicero a now lost treatise on grammar, *De Analogia*, written while he was travelling across the Alps after the Luca conference in 56, and later remarked that Cicero had won greater laurels in extending the boundaries of Roman genius than any general in extending the frontiers of the empire. He also made a collection of Cicero's jokes, from which he rigidly excluded any that he did not know to be genuine.

ROME 47 BC

There was some chaos to be sorted out when Caesar finally got back to Rome. There had been no elections for 47. He had two of his officers elected consuls for the remaining weeks of the year, and himself for 46, in conjunction with Lepidus. Antony, in the course of a year in which he had virtually held absolute power, was temporarily out of favour with Caesar for using too much force to quell a mob protesting about the policy towards debts. Caesar made Lepidus *magister equitum* instead and did what he could by legislation to resolve the debt problem. His crack legion, the Tenth, having marched from Greece the previous year, camped outside the city demanding back pay and their discharge if they did not get it. He faced them alone. Since he did not have the funds, he implied that they were thus free to go. He would, however, still pay them when he had finished the present business without them.

KEY FACT

It was probably during his short stay in Rome in 47 that Caesar arranged for the publication of his second volume of military memoirs, *De Bello Civili* ('Civil War'). Covering the events of January 49 to September 48, it was designed largely to justify Caesar's actions.

The booty from the campaign would be distributed among the rest of the army.

There was little time to spare, for the Pompeians were massing in force in Africa. Caesar needed the men of the Tenth as much as they needed him. To a man they withdrew their demands. Caesar was, however, inflexible where military discipline was concerned. He saw to it that for the remainder of his campaign against the Pompeians, the Tenth was always sent into the most lethal situations.

CIVIL WAR – THIRD PHASE, AFRICA 46 BC

The Pompeians had formed ten new legions. Juba, still nursing his implacable hatred of Caesar, contributed a further four Numidian legions, trained in the Roman style of warfare. There was also a complement of 15,000 cavalry. As commander, possibly out of respect to Pompey, they elected his father-in-law, Quintus Metellus Scipio. The vastly experienced Labienus was second-in-command.

Caesar's initial expeditionary force consisted of five of his newer legions and one, the Fifth, which had been with him since the war in Gaul. Because of the winter gales, they had to be sent in instalments from Marsala in Sicily to the African coast in the region of Leptis. It is said that just as Caesar himself set foot on dry land, he tripped and fell flat on his face. Those present were aghast at this apparently worst of omens. With great presence of mind, Caesar stretched out his arms, gripped the ground, kissed it, and exclaimed, 'Ha, I've got you, Africa!'

Early progress was slow, and Caesar sent for further experienced legions, including the Tenth. The final showdown came at Thapsus. By a combined land/sea operation, Caesar managed to draw Scipio into forming up in battle formation, with a squadron of Juba's elephants on each wing. Caesar's plan was to deploy his troops in three lines as at Pharsalus, with detachments of the Fifth Legion, who had demanded this privilege, behind each wing in oblique formation to deal with the elephants. He was still arranging the disposition of his troops when someone trumpeted the charge. In the chaos, Scipio's elephants ran amok and trampled to death many of his own troops. Caesar's soldiers butchered most of the rest.

Some of Scipio's cavalry fled to Utica, which was administered by Cato. They forced their way into the town, massacred many of its inhabitants and looted buildings. Cato had to bribe them to depart. Then, rather than give Caesar the satisfaction of accepting his surrender, he arranged his personal and civic affairs, and killed himself. Other leaders of his movement were hunted down or committed suicide. Caesar's policy with prisoners was to spare them if they had not been captured before, but to kill them if they had been taken for the second time. He established colonies along the coast in which to settle some of his veterans. In June he crossed with the rest of his troops to Sardinia, where he weeded out prospective trouble-makers among them who might mutiny, and despatched them as reinforcements to Spain, where

Pompey's two sons were keeping alive their father's memory. To the Fifth Legion Caesar awarded the unique accolade of an elephant as its permanent emblem.

QUADRUPLE TRIUMPH

Caesar's return to Rome in July 46 was the signal for unprecedented jubilation and a flood of honours. He was appointed dictator for ten years. He was granted a fourfold triumph for his victories over Gaul, the Egyptians, Pharnaces, and Numidia – those over fellow Romans were diplomatically ignored. A bronze statue of Caesar astride the known world was commissioned, with an inscription to the effect that he was a demigod – he later had this quietly erased. He was given the title of 'Controller of Public Morals'. More significantly, it was decreed that he should sit in the senate beside the consuls and have the right always to speak first on any issue.

His triumph was held over four days, and began with the worst of omens. The axle of his chariot broke as it was passing the Temple of Fortune, depositing him in the road. Another one was sent for and, in order to demonstrate his humility, he climbed up the steps at the temple on the Capitol Hill on his knees.

The crowds had a great time. They saw Arsinoe led in by chains, and also Vercingetorix who, having served his purpose, was taken away and strangled. The veteran legions who had served in Gaul paraded past, happily chanting rude marching songs:

> Caesar celebrates a triumph:
>   Nicomedes, bugger all!
> Nicomedes buggered Caesar:
>   Caesar buggered Gaul!

> Suetonius, *Julius Caesar* 49

And:

> Lock up your wives, inhabitants of Rome,
>> His army brings the bald adulterer home.
> The gold he borrowed for his Gallic wars,
>> He spent instead upon his Gallic whores.

Suetonius, Julius Caesar 51

There was prize-money for the troops, and a public feast for which 22,000 tables were laid, groaning with food. Afterwards Caesar was escorted home by elephants carrying torches, and by what seemed to be the whole populace. Then there were the games, for days on end. Gladiators fought to the death, actors performed on mobile stages, athletes ran and wrestled against each other. There was a big-game hunt which went on for five days, during which 400 lions were slaughtered and 50 elephants were goaded into fighting each other. There were sea fights on a specially constructed lake, and a land battle to the death between two armies of condemned criminals and prisoners-of-war. And to cap it all, the public of Rome were treated for the first time to the sight of a giraffe, which they called a 'cameleopard'.

Not everyone appreciated Caesar's lavishness. Some of his veterans felt that some of the money might have been better spent as bonuses to them. To put a stop once and for all to potential mutinies, Caesar approached one of the protesters, grabbed him, and handed him over for instant execution. Two others, by way of ritual observance, were ordered to be publicly sacrificed and their heads strung up outside Caesar's official residence as *pontifex maximus*.

KEY FACT

Human sacrifice was not a Roman practice. Only three previous instances have been recorded, in 228, 216 and 114 BC. The last of these was instigated by a flash of lightning which struck a vestal virgin. A special commission, set up to investigate the phenomenon, convicted by dubious means several other vestals of sexual practices. To avert public hysteria, the senate called for a reading from the Sibylline Books, the national storehouse of prophetic lore. The answer came to bury alive a Greek and a Gallic couple.

There were now certain administrative reforms to be attended to, of which Caesar informed the senate when it suited him to do so. Otherwise he simply used the names of prominent senators without their knowledge as supporters of a bill. Cicero was amused to receive letters from foreign kings of whose existence he was unaware, thanking him for proposing them for their royal title.

Caesar made Roman citizenship more accessible to those people who had been defeated or whose territory had been annexed. He increased the number of senators from 600 to 900, and made the centre of government more of a 'people's senate' by recruiting members from the provinces and from Italian communities. He also introduced a fast track system whereby a man could be promoted to a higher rank without having served at a lower level. He held a census and reduced the number of those entitled to the corn dole. Members of juries now had to be equestrians or senators. There were restrictions on the purchase of some luxury goods. Incentives were available for large families. Political clubs masquerading as guilds were banned. The burden on debtors was reduced.

Of lasting significance was Caesar's reform of the calendar, which had been based on the lunar year and had got into such a tangle during the civil war that mid-summer fell in September. With the help of Sosigenes, Cleopatra's astronomer, he devised a new calendar based on the solar year, similar to that which operated in Egypt, but with improvements. It enabled the agricultural year to be reconciled with the duration of a complete revolution of the moon around the earth, while disturbing as little as possible what were traditionally the special days of the month. It was a brilliant performance, on the part of someone who was able to grasp the boundaries of astronomical science.

The Egyptians had 12 months of 30 days each, and made up the year by adding an extra five days at its end. Caesar arrived at his year of $365\frac{1}{4}$ days by distributing these five days, plus two that he deducted from February, among seven months; he made up the whole day which accrued from the accumulation of quarters by adding it to February every fourth year. In acknowledgment of his contribution, he agreed that the month in which his birthday fell, the fifth month of the year by the original calendar, which until 153 BC began in March, should be called July in his honour. Cicero was not impressed. When someone observed that the constellation of Lyra would rise the following night, he quipped, 'Yes, by official dispensation!'

KEY FACT

The priests misinterpreted Caesar's instructions about the leap year, as a result of which a correction had to be made in the time of Augustus. Otherwise, apart from a further adjustment by Pope Gregory XIII in the sixteenth century, the calendar in force today is that devised by Julius Caesar in 46 BC.

In order that the new Julian calendar could be implemented on 1 January 45, Caesar allowed for the statutory intercalary month of 23 days at the end of February 46, and inserted two extra months of 33 and 34 days between November and December 46.

While all this frantic public business was being conducted, Cleopatra arrived in Rome for a state visit, accompanied by her 12-year-old husband and her one-year-old son by Caesar. Caesar was charmed and had a statue of her placed beside that of the goddess in the temple of Venus Genetrix. Roman society was scandalized. Caesar took no notice. Indeed, according to the third-century AD historian, Dio Cassius, the Egyptian royal family stayed in Caesar's house. Calpurnia's views are not recorded.

KEY FACT

Genetrix means mother, and traditionally Venus was the mother of Aeneas, mythological founder of the Roman race. According to the historian Appian, the statue of Cleopatra was still there over 200 years later.

Caesar was also desperately anxious to get back to Spain, where Pompey's son, also Gnaeus, with the assistance of his younger brother Sextus and of Labienus, who had survived the fighting in Africa, were raising new forces. Their determination was fuelled by several years of mismanagement by the Roman governor of the province. The two legates whom Caesar had put in charge of the military operation were being hard pressed to maintain any sort of order.

CIVIL WAR – FOURTH PHASE, SPAIN 45 BC

According to near contemporary reports, Caesar arrived on the scene before either his opponents or even his own men knew he was on the way. It appears that he made the journey from Rome almost to Corduba, a distance of 2,400 km, in 27 days. To do this, he must have travelled by carriage ahead of his legions. These included the Fifth, and also the Tenth, which had been disbanded after Thapsus and now brought back again into service with, as its basis, former soldiers of the legion who had been settled in Arelate and Narbo, on Caesar's route to Spain.

The campaign, fought during the winter, was hard and bloody. It was concluded at Munda. Against his opponents' 11 legions and several thousand cavalry and light-armed auxiliaries, Caesar had eight legions, supported by auxiliaries and cavalry, among which was a squadron commanded by Bogud, king of Mauretania.

At the height of the battle, the unthinkable happened. With the two sides locked together and bent on cutting each other down, Caesar's veteran legions began to give way, until a gap appeared between the two opposing armies. Caesar jumped from his horse, threw off his helmet to make sure that his men recognized him, grabbed a shield and ran in front of his

Caesar is said to have had at one time an affair with Bogud's wife, Eunoe, and to have rewarded the king handsomely for the experience.

own line, shouting to anyone who could hear, 'This is the end of me and of your army service!' As he stood firm, evading javelins or catching them on his shield, his military tribunes ran forward and formed up beside him. The legions rallied. It was reported that Caesar later admitted that he had often fought for victory, but this time it was for his life; indeed, when he saw his soldiers retreat, he considered killing himself.

The situation was finally saved, as on previous occasions, by the Tenth Legion who, from their privileged position on the right of the line, broke up the opposition's left wing, and by a brilliant move by Bogud and his cavalry. Caesar, master of Rome, was now master of the Roman empire, and effectively of the world.

The Ides of March 44 BC

6

*Many will confirm this story. A certain soothsayer warned Caesar
to beware of great danger on the day of March that the Romans
call the Ides. When the day came, and Caesar was on his way to
the senate-house, he made a joke of it, and said to the man, 'Well,
this is the Ides of March.' At which the soothsayer whispered to
him, 'Indeed, the day has come, but it's not over yet.'*

Plutarch, *Caesar* LXIII, 6

The battle of Munda was in March 45. Caesar, having sorted out to his
satisfaction the situation in Spain, attended to some personal business
and arrived back in Rome in October 45. The frenetic activity now
began again, interspersed with some out-of-town social visits. Caesar's
niece Atia had married, as her second husband, Lucius Marcius
Philippus, who had a villa near Puteoli. Caesar went to stay with them
for the Saturnalia in December, accompanied
by an entourage of 2,000, including a troop of
armed cavalry. On the second day of the
holiday he went over to see Cicero in one of the
latter's several country houses. Cicero was
obliged not only to give dinner to his
distinguished guest, but also to feed, in three
other dining-rooms, his attendants. In a letter
to his friend Atticus, Cicero admitted that he
quite enjoyed himself, but that Caesar was not
the kind of guest to whom one says, 'Do come
again next time you are in this area,' and added,
'Once is enough!'

KEY FACT

Titus Pomponius Atticus
(109–32 BC) was a good
friend to Cicero and his
family. After Cicero's
death he edited four
collections of letters
Cicero had written to
him between 68 and 44
BC. Cicero was a prolific
writer of letters, many of
which were intended for
publication.

In Rome there had been plentiful honours and plaudits. Caesar was
made dictator for life, consul for ten years, and granted, as a hereditary

title, the permanent accolade of *imperator*. An additional temple to Libertas, goddess of freedom, was to be erected in his honour. An ivory statue of Caesar was to be carried along with those of the gods in the procession which inaugurated each occasion of the games. A further statue was to be set up in the temple dedicated to Romulus, founder of the city, with the inscription, 'To the invincible god', and yet another one on the Capitol alongside those of the former kings of Rome. It was precisely gestures such as these which Caesar's enemies

> **KEY FACT**
>
> *Imperator* was a title of honour conferred on a victorious general, and could be granted several times to the same man. The term is related to *imperium*, the literal meaning of which is akin to both 'command' and 'power'. In time, *imperator* came to mean 'emperor'.

found tactless, if not also distasteful, and they registered their disapproval by voting against them in the senate – it is recorded that Caesar did not question their right to do so.

There was an unfortunate incident when, after a day in which an unusually large number of honours had been debated and approved by an overwhelming margin, representatives of the senate went to Caesar, who was sitting in the vestibule of the temple of Venus, to tell him the good news. He received the deputation without rising from his chair of state, an offence to protocol of the first magnitude. Some people tried to excuse him on the grounds that he had an attack of diarrhoea and could not stand up in case he was taken short. They obviously did not see him, soon afterwards, get to his feet and walk home.

His arrogance on this occasion was held more heinous because of another incident during the triumphal procession which he insisted on holding for his victories in Spain, though these were over other Roman citizens. One of the tribunes of the people, Pontius Aquila, stayed firmly in his seat as Caesar's chariot passed. Caesar shouted at him, 'Come on, Aquila, are you trying to get me to restore the republic?' Caesar later retaliated in his jokey fashion. For several days afterwards, any undertaking he gave was qualified with the words, 'If Pontius Aquila pleases!'

Staunch republicans were further disgusted by Caesar's ambivalent attitude to those who wished to dub him 'king'. Caesar would go through the motions of refusing the title, even to the extent of rebuking people who linked him with it, but without showing any genuine displeasure at the idea. It was thus perhaps inevitable that someone should place a crown on his statue. Two of the tribunes removed it and brought a prosecution against the man alleged to be the first to call Caesar 'king'. Caesar expressed great resentment at their actions. When the tribunes complained that their freedom of speech was being infringed, Caesar lost his temper, hauled them into the senate-house and had them removed from office. As the persons and actions of the tribunes were sacrosanct, this was an act of gross lese-majesty.

Matters came to a head at the fertility festival of the Lupercalia in February. Proceedings used to begin in the cave where Romulus and Remus, the mythical founders of Rome, were supposed to have been suckled by a wolf. Some goats and a dog were sacrificed and the blood smeared over two youths of aristocratic birth, who then ran a prescribed cross-country course, carrying strips of hide, with which they whipped people as they passed. The blows were supposed to promote fertility, and women who wanted to become pregnant would place themselves at strategic points on the course. On this occasion, Antony, who was back in favour with Caesar and was his colleague as consul for the year, insisted on being one of the runners, though one would have thought he was a bit old for that sort of caper. He must at least have been slightly out of breath when at the end of the course he produced a crown, which he formally offered to Caesar on behalf of the people of Rome. Caesar refused it, but the damage had been done.

Caesar was de facto king in all but name. His driving ambition and sheer energy had precipitated too many fundamental changes too quickly, without there being realistic substitutes in place for the traditions he was sweeping away. This is a problem still in modern times.

THE PLOT

It is probable that several groups of people had been thinking about the idea of assassination – there is even a suggestion that Antony had been sounded out a year before, but had kept the information to himself. The instigator of the final plot was Gaius Cassius Longinus, who had a distinguished record as a public servant and soldier. He had fought for Pompey and, along with Marcus Brutus, had been pardoned by Caesar, who had him appointed to a praetorship in 44. Cassius's initial motives may have been purely personal. A bitter man, he had never forgiven Caesar for appropriating some lions which Cassius had acquired in Megara for showing at the games which he would be presenting during his year as aedile.

The other principal plotter was Marcus Brutus himself, a man steeped in the political philosophy of Cato. His wife Porcia, Cato's daughter, is said to have been the only woman to have been let into the secret. Guessing from her husband's mood that something was going on, and believing that she would not be told about it unless she proved herself able to keep quiet even under torture, she stabbed herself in the thigh. She then went to Brutus and showed him the deep gash, whereupon he told her everything.

There were in all about 60 conspirators, comprising discontented officials, former soldiers, and members of the senate. Two, Gaius Trebonius and Decimus Junius Brutus, had held very senior positions in Caesar's army, and were trusted by him. Decimus had been promised the governorship of Cisalpine Gaul, and a consulship in 42. The conspirators' watchword was 'freedom', and their credo the convention in the ancient world that to kill a tyrant was an acceptable practice. Their mistake was to assume that if they killed Caesar, everything would carry on without him as before. They decided that to assassinate Antony as well would be unwarranted; besides he was an elected consul. That was their second mistake.

What brought the plot to a head was Caesar's announcement that on 18 March he would be off to lead the army which was marching against the Parthians, to avenge the killing of Crassus. Otherwise, nothing might ever have come of it, because the conspirators were still in awe of the man's achievements and his charm. The plot itself, with so many people involved, seems to have been an unguarded secret. When someone spitefully told Caesar that Antony and Publius Cornelius Dolabella, Cicero's profligate son-in-law, were up to no good, he observed, 'It's not the long-haired fatties that bother me, but the pale, thin ones' – a clear reference to Brutus and Cassius. He dispensed with his Spanish personal security guards, saying, 'There is nothing worse than than always being on the look-out for something; that is a sign of one who is perpetually afraid.' The biographer Suetonius, writing about 150 years afterwards, suggests that Caesar, who was now in his 56th year, had a death-wish, brought on by failing health. Certainly Caesar had suffered what appears to have been one of his epileptic fits before the battle of Thapsus a year earlier.

The conspirators settled on 15 March, the day known as the Ides of March, when Caesar was due to meet members of the senate in a hall off the theatre of Pompey. On 14 March, Caesar was dining at the house of Lepidus and was, as usual, signing documents while reclining at the table, when the conversation turned to what was the best kind of death. Before anyone could speak, Caesar, without looking up from what he was doing, called out, 'Sudden death!'

That night, when he was in bed with his wife, all the windows and doors of the room burst open simultaneously. Caesar started up. In the light of the moon he saw Calpurnia was still soundly asleep, but she was talking indistinctly to herself

KEY FACT

The months were divided into three sections, each being indicated by a special day. The Calends was always the first day of the month. The Ides was the notional day of the full moon, 15 March, 15 May, 15 July and 15 October, and the 13th day of the other months. The Nones was the ninth day before the Ides, including the day at each end of the period.

and groaning. The next morning she said that she had dreamed that she was holding the body of her murdered husband in her arms. She begged him not to go to the meeting.

Caesar, by Roman standards, was not a superstitious person, but then neither was Calpurnia, who now suggested he should get a second opinion. The official augurs went through their rituals several times, always with the same sinister results. Caesar made up his mind to skip the meeting, and asked Antony to inform the senate that it had been cancelled.

Brutus and Cassius were most agitated when they heard the news. Was their cover blown? If not, would they get another chance before Caesar left for the wars? They sent Decimus Brutus, whom, after Antony and Lepidus, Caesar trusted most, to persuade him to change his mind. At least, Decimus explained to Caesar, if this was an unlucky day on which to do public business, he should still go to the meeting and formally adjourn it. While talking, he took Caesar by the hand and imperceptibly led him out into the street.

As usual, Caesar was besieged along the way by people handing him petitions on little rolls of paper, which he would immediately pass to a secretary following behind. However, when Artemidorus, a teacher of philosophy who knew what the conspirators were up to, approached him with a roll and whispered, 'Please read this yourself, and now, it concerns you personally,' Caesar kept hold of it, but was unable to look at it in the press of people.

Antony was waiting at the entrance to the hall, but was prevented from accompanying Caesar inside by Trebonius, who engaged him in conversation. As Caesar entered, the senators rose to their feet. Some of the conspirators congregated behind the seat on which Caesar would sit; others joined Tillius Cimber, who was making a great show of greeting Caesar with a petition on behalf of his exiled brother. Caesar sat down, protesting that he had come to adjourn the meeting. Cimber took hold of Caesar's toga at the neck with both hands, and pulled it from his shoulders. This was the signal for the attack.

It was so furious that in the confusion several senators knifed each other. After it, there were 23 stab wounds in Caesar's body, though a doctor later stated that only the second, to the chest, was fatal.

The conspirators rushed to barricade themselves in the temple on Capitol Hill and awaited the upsurge of public support that they felt they had earned. The senators who were not in the plot, scattered. Members of Caesar's personal entourage fled. Three slaves put Caesar's body in a litter and carried it back to the house, staggering unsteadily, as the litter was designed to be supported by four men. Antony, as the senior official in the state, took charge, and ordered Lepidus to bring into the city troops which he had at his disposal. From a grieving Calpurnia, he obtained Caesar's personal papers relating to the state. Then he called a meeting of the senate for 17 March.

THE REACTION

During the night after the murder, Cicero, who had not been a party to the plot, but heartily approved of it, visited the conspirators. The next day, Brutus and Cassius ventured out into the streets to address a mob which had been bribed to respond favourably. Their appearance was given some sense of authority by the presence of Dolabella, whom Caesar, in his absence on the Parthian trail, had nominated as substitute consul for the rest of the year.

Antony prepared the ground well. Though the senatorial members of the plot were invited to attend the meeting, they prudently decided to stay away. There was much animated debate about their status. If Caesar were officially to be declared a tyrant, then his assassins could claim immunity. Antony intervened. If Caesar were a tyrant, then *ipso facto* all his actions and all the appointments he had made were automatically cancelled. This brought the meeting to its senses. Dolabella, who had been consul for less than 48 hours, changed his allegiance and supported the status quo. Cicero, though it went against the grain, proposed that all Caesar's actions should be ratified, but that there should be no reprisals against his murderers. It was, in a way, a victory for order, if not also for law.

Caesar's will contained a number of surprises. The principal beneficiary was Gaius Octavius, his 18-year-old great-nephew, Atia's son by her first marriage, and the grandson of his sister Julia (minor). Gaius Octavius was also adopted as Caesar's son, assuming the name of Gaius Julius Caesar Octavianus (Octavian). The rest of Caesar's residuary estate was left to his other great-nephews, Quintus Pedius, who had served as one of Caesar's legates in Spain in 46, and Lucius Pinarius. Several of the conspirators, most notably Decimus Brutus, were also named. To the citizens of Rome he bequeathed in perpetuity his gardens by the River Tiber, and three hundred sesterces each, the equivalent of four months' basic pay for a legionary.

Caesar's body was publicly cremated in the Forum. Antony said a few words chosen to incite the people against the murderers. He succeeded so well that the mob mistook Helvius Cinna, poet and also tribune in 44, for the praetor Cornelius Cinna, who had spoken out against Caesar, and tore him to pieces so conclusively that no part of him was ever found for burial. At that, the assassins quit the city, Brutus and Cassius for a brief nomadic existence in Italy. Decimus Brutus departed for Cisalpine Gaul, as governor of which he had, extraordinarily, been confirmed by the senate.

After the funeral many came to the Forum to pay their respects to Caesar's memory. Principal among them were members of Rome's Jewish community, some of whom returned several nights in a row to stand around the remains of the pyre, and to say their own prayers for the dead.

What Happened Next?

7

When more accurate information about the murder of Caesar was available, Octavian's mother and stepfather warned him strongly to watch his step. They even suggested he should renounce both his adoption and his inheritance. His response was that to do so, and take no reprisals against those responsible for Caesar's death, would be unthinkable.

Appian, *The Civil Wars* III, 11

Octavian, who was in Apollonia pursuing his military studies when Caesar was murdered, returned to Rome to claim his *imperium* at the end of April 44. There was a confrontation with Antony, who saw himself, rather than this teenage hypochondriac, as the rightful successor to Caesar's authority, as well as to Caesar's fortune.

Brutus and Cassius, to whom the senate had allocated the governorships respectively of Crete and Cyrene, protested that these appointments were beneath them. When the senate took no notice, they left Italy in a huff to drum up military support in the east. Antony, who had been allocated Macedonia, had a law passed giving him instead Cisalpine and Transalpine Gaul for five years, and transferring Caesar's legions from Macedonia to his new provinces. The senate, at the instigation of Cicero, advised Decimus Brutus to stay put until further notice. Octavian quietly gathered military support, in the charismatic name of Caesar. Cicero now made a series of blistering speeches in the senate accusing Antony of all kinds of misdemeanours.

Antony stayed in Rome only to hear the first. Without waiting even for Decimus Brutus's original year of office to end, he marched his legions into the province and shut Decimus Brutus up in Mutina. The senate despatched the consuls for 43, Aulus Hirtius and Gaius Vibius Pansa, with an army to deal with the emergency. Octavian joined up with them and together they defeated Antony, though Hirtius was killed in action and Pansa died shortly afterwards of his wounds. Decimus Brutus emerged from Mutina with his troops, who then deserted him. He met his death at the hands of a Gallic chief.

Octavian now demanded that he be appointed to one of the two vacant consulships. The senate refused. Octavian marched on Rome with his troops and effectively took over the city. He insisted on elections, at which he and his cousin Pedius were returned as consuls. He then joined forces with Antony and Lepidus and had a bill pushed through giving the three of them responsibility for re-establishing the constitution for a period of five years – their rule is known as the Second Triumvirate.

They resolved the problems of cash and of those whom they saw as inimical to the state by re-introducing the fearful proscriptions such as had marked the rule of Sulla. According to Appian, 300 senators and 2,000 equestrians were listed to be killed and to have their properties confiscated. Among them was Cicero, who met his end courageously. His head and right hand were then cut off and sent to Antony, who had them nailed up in the Forum.

The triumvirate nominally remained in control for 12 turbulent years. Brutus and Cassius were defeated at Philippi in Macedonia in 42, and committed suicide. Sextus Pompey, having inherited his father's naval skills and taken Sicily, was murdered by his own troops in 35. Lepidus was gradually eased into the background. Antony's fatal attraction for Cleopatra, in preference to his wife Octavia, who was Octavian's sister, was his final undoing. Octavian outmanoeuvred the Egyptian fleet at Actium in 31. Antony killed himself. The 36-year-old Cleopatra, after failing in an attempt to vamp Octavian (24), applied poisonous snakes to her veins, and died. Octavian allowed her two children with Antony to survive, but had Caesarion murdered.

Octavian was now in charge of the Roman world, a position he kept for over 40 years. In 27 BC he formally traded in what had effectively been a military dictatorship for special powers, and transferred the nominal management of affairs of state to the senate and to the Roman people. He also assumed the more dignified name of Augustus.

8 Julius Caesar, Achievements and Legacy

> *'What words can match the greatness of his deeds?'*
> Mark Antony, quoted in Dio Cassius, *Roman History* XLIV, 36

No head of state in ancient or modern times applied himself so assiduously as did Caesar to such a wide range of activities, and excelled at all of them. As statesman and general he has been compared with Oliver Cromwell. Winston Churchill may rank alongside him as a historical writer, without having Caesar's intellectual grasp. As a politician, Caesar completed the transition from a republican system which did not work, to something approaching a monarchy, which worked for a time under the successor he chose and the dynasty he founded, and later in the hands of emperors such as Trajan, Hadrian and Marcus Aurelius. Without Caesar there would have been no Augustan Age in Rome, or possibly anywhere else. And Caesar's mistresses were probably more numerous, and certainly classier, than those of any modern statesman or politician.

Caesar increased the number of Roman provinces from 14 to 17. He extended the franchise to those of non-Roman birth, and made membership of the senate more accessible. He reduced overcrowding in Rome by encouraging emigration to Roman colonies abroad, which he established also for the settlement of retired soldiers. He ordered the census to be taken not just in Rome, but simultaneously throughout Italy, with a view to extending it to all parts of the Roman empire. He worked out methods of codifying Roman law, which were not acted upon for another 500 years. His toleration of non-Roman religious faiths was more understanding than that of any of his successors.

Caesar was an inspirational military strategist, even if he did nothing to revolutionize prevailing military tactics. He succeeded time and time again, even when Romans were fighting Romans, because of his instinctive grasp of a situation, his quickness of mind and his qualities of leadership.

Though he spent hardly any of his last 15 years at the centre of government in Rome, Caesar tackled the problems of debt, poverty, and the mismanagement of affairs in the provinces. He attended to public works and drew up plans for draining the Pomptine marshes and Lake Fucinus. He relieved the chronic traffic congestion in Rome by forbidding the movement of wheeled vehicles in the city from sunrise until dusk. He planned a public library, under the directorship of Marcus Terentius Varro (116–28 BC), the finest scholar and archivist of the day. His educational reforms also included granting Roman citizenship to all foreign teachers of liberal arts, as well as medical practitioners, domiciled in Rome or wishing to settle there in the future.

As well as his calendar, he gave to the modern world the obstetrical term 'Caesarean section', from the fact that he is reputed to have been born in that fashion. It may be that Caesar has been better remembered for the manner of his death than for what he did in his lifetime. His assassination, however, inspired one of Shakespeare's best, and most frequently performed, historical plays, based on Sir Thomas North's translation (1597), from the French, of Plutarch's *Lives*. With an astonishing stroke of perception, Shakespeare makes Cassius say, after the murder of Caesar, 'How many ages hence / Shall this our lofty scene be acted over / In states unborn and accents yet unknown!' (*Julius Caesar*, III, i, 111–13).

Table of Dates (BC)

100 Birth of Julius Caesar.

88 First consulship of Sulla.

86 Death of Marius.

85 Death of Caesar's father.

84 Caesar marries Cornelia. Appointed priest of Jupiter.

82 Sulla appointed dictator.

81 Caesar in Asia.

79 Death of Sulla.

77 Caesar prosecutes Dolabella.

74 Caesar in Rhodes and Asia.

73 Caesar in Rome. Appointed to pontifical college.

70 First consulship of Crassus and Pompey.

69 Death of Cornelia.

68 Caesar is quaestor in Spain.

66 Caesar marries Pompeia.

65 Caesar is aedile.

63 Catiline conspiracy. Caesar elected *pontifex maximus.*

62 Caesar elected praetor. The 'Bona Dea' affair. Caesar divorces Pompeia.

61 Caesar in Spain.

60 First triumvirate of Caesar, Crassus and Pompey.

59 Caesar's first consulship, and appointed governor of Gaul for five years. Marriage to Calpurnia.

58 Battle of Bibracte.

57 Caesar defeats Belgae.

56 Renewal of first triumvirate.

55 Caesar's governorship renewed for five years. He crosses Rhine. First invasion of Britain.

54 Second invasion of Britain. Death of Caesar's daughter.

53 Death of Crassus.

52 Battle of Alesia. Capture of Vercingetorix.

51 End of Gallic wars. Attempts to end Caesar's command.
    Publication of *De Bello Gallico*.
49 Caesar crosses Rubicon. Pompey appointed dictator. Civil war.
    Caesar in Spain. Battle of Ilerda. Caesar appointed dictator.
    Elected consul for 48.
48 Battles of Dyrrachium and Pharsalus. Death of Pompey.
    Caesar in Egypt with Cleopatra. Fighting in Alexandria.
    Caesar reappointed dictator.
47 Battle of Zela. Caesar returns to Rome. Publication of
    De Bello Civili.
46 Battle of Thapsus. Caesar appointed dictator for ten years and
    holds quadruple triumph. He reforms the calendar. Cleopatra
    in Rome.
45 Battle of Munda, final defeat of Pompey supporters.
44 Caesar appointed dictator for life, 14 February.
    Assassinated, 15 March.

FURTHER READING

Biographies

Major-General J. F. C Fuller, *Julius Caesar: Man, Soldier, and Tyrant*,
new edition, Wordsworth Editions (1998). Excellent, as one might
expect, on the military side, and documented with sources.

Christian Meier, *Caesar*, translated from the German by David
McLintock, paperback edition, Fontana (1996). Long and detailed.
The omission of sources makes it difficult to judge how much may
be speculation.

Pat Southern, *Julius Caesar*, Tempus (2001). Short, well told,
strong on the political side.

Alan Massie, *Caesar*, paperback edition, Sceptre (1994).
A historical novel as told by Decimus Brutus, with cracking
dialogue.

Translations

Julius Caesar, *De Bello Gallico*: as *The Conquest of Gaul*,
translated by Jane F. Gardner, reissue Penguin (1982); as *The
Gallic War*, translated by Carolyn Hammond, Oxford University
Press (1996).

Julius Caesar, *De Bello Civili*: as *The Civil War*, translated by
Jane F. Mitchell, Penguin (1996); translated by J. M. Carter, Oxford
University Press (1997).

Suetonius, *The Twelve Caesars*, translated by Robert Graves,
revised and introduced by Michael Grant, Penguin (1979).

Background Studies

Anthony Everitt, *Cicero: a Turbulent Life*, John Murray (2001).

Peter Jones and Keith C. Sidwell, *The World of Rome: an introduction to Roman culture*, Cambridge University Press (1997).

Antony Kamm, *The Romans: an introduction*, fourth printing, with revisions, Routledge (1999).

Lawrence Keppie, *The Making of the Roman Army: from Republic to Empire*, new edition Routledge (1998).

David Shotter, *The Fall of the Roman Republic*, Routledge (1994).

Pat Southern, *Augustus*, Routledge (2001); *Cleopatra*, Tempus (1999); *Mark Antony*, Tempus (1998).

Richard Stoneman, *Alexander the Great*, Routledge (1997).

INDEX